Lucy in the Sky

Lucy in the Sky

Anonymous

Simon Pulse

New York   London   Toronto   Sydney   New Delhi

SIMON PULSE

An imprint of Simon & Schuster Children's Publishing Division

1230 Avenue of the Americas, New York, NY 10020

First Simon Pulse edition May 2012

Copyright © 2012 by Simon & Schuster, Inc.

All rights reserved, including the right of reproduction in whole or in part in any form.

SIMON PULSE and colophon are registered trademarks of Simon & Schuster, Inc.

For information about special discounts for bulk purchases, please contact Simon & Schuster Special Sales at 1-866-506-1949 or business@simonandschuster.com.

The Simon & Schuster Speakers Bureau can bring authors to your live event. For more information or to book an event contact the Simon & Schuster Speakers Bureau at 1-866-248-3049 or visit our website at www.simonspeakers.com.

The text of this book was set in Adobe Caslon Pro.

Manufactured in the United States of America

10 9 8 7 6

Library of Congress Control Number 2012930474

ISBN 978-1-4424-5187-2 (hc)

ISBN 978-1-4424-5185-8 (pbk)

ISBN 978-1-4424-5188-9 (eBook)

Lucy in the Sky

July 4

Dear Diary,

That's ridiculous. Who writes "Dear Diary" in a diary? I mean, who writes in a diary at all? Shouldn't I be blogging?

This is lame.

July 5

Okay, so this isn't going to be a diary. It's a journal. I guess that's the same thing, but "journal" sounds less like I'm riding a tricycle or something.

Yesterday was my birthday. I turned 16.

It's so weird sharing a birthday with your country. Always fireworks: never for you. Mom always plans an actual birthday dinner—usually the Saturday night after July 4th so that I can have a day where we celebrate just for me. It's fun, kinda like having two birthdays in the same week.

We're not big July 4th celebrators . . . celebrators? Celebrants? People. Whatever—we're not big on July 4th. Usually in the afternoon we have friends from school over and walk down to the beach to play volleyball. There are lots of nets at the beach just down the hill, then we haul ourselves back up the canyon to our house for a cookout in the evening. My brother, Cam, invites his friends from the varsity soccer team. Mom gets my favorite cake (the one with the berries in it).

After we gorge on grilled meat and birthday cake, we all crowd onto the balcony outside my parents' bedroom and watch the fireworks down the coast. You can see the display at the pier really well, and the ones in the cities just up the coast shoot off too. Last year Cam (nobody calls him Cameron except Mom) climbed onto the roof from the front porch so he could get a better view, but Mom freaked and said, CAMERON! Get. Down. This. Instant. Mom's big on safety.

I got a lot of cool presents yesterday. Mom got me the swimsuit I tried on at the mall last week. It's a really cute two-piece with boy shorts, and this fun, twisty top. Dad's present to me was that he's taking me to get my license this week. I've been practicing with him in the parking lot near his office at the college. He gave me a coupon for one "Full Day with Dad." On the back it says, "Good for one driving test at the DMV, followed by a celebratory meal at the restaurant of holder's choosing, and a $100 shopping spree/gift card to store of choice."

He made it himself out of red construction paper and drew this funny little stick figure on the front. It's supposed to be him. He draws curly hair on the sides of the round head so the little man is bald on top like he is. The coupon is sort of cheesy, but so is my dad. I think it's funny. And cute.

Cam got me this journal. We've been going to this yoga

2

class together, and the teacher is this woman named Marty with bright eyes who talks about her birds a lot. She told us to get a journal and spend a few minutes each day writing down our thoughts and feelings.

I just looked back at everything I've written, and it's mainly thoughts. Not very many feelings. I'm not sure how I feel right now. I mean, I guess I feel fine? Happy?

No, just fine. I feel fine.

I also feel like people who have birds are sort of weird.

July 6

It's funny that Cam bought me this journal. It's one of those things I would never have bought for myself but secretly wanted. I don't know how he knows that stuff. I guess that's what older brothers are supposed to do: read your mind. I mean, who actually goes out and tries the stuff that their yoga teacher says to do outside of class?

Cam got way into yoga last summer when he had a crush on this exchange student from England named Briony—like Brian with a y. (Really? Who names their kid that?) Anyway, she wouldn't give Cam the time of day, so when he found out that she went to this yoga class, he started going to the same one. He bought a mat and this little bag to carry it in and just happened to show up in her class like, Oh my God! Wow!

What a coincidence. Briony never went out with him. I didn't even know she'd gone back to London until I was teasing him about how he should be glad Briony didn't do something like synchronized swimming. He was like, Briony moved back to London right after school got out.

I asked him why he was still going to yoga, and he said he really liked it. And he said I should come.

I'm not sure why I did, really. I guess I was just bored last summer. But now we go to yoga together. It's this really great studio a block off the Promenade, and they run it on donations. You just pay what you can or what you think the class is worth. I didn't think I'd like it at first. It was hard, and I got sweaty and slipped on my mat and couldn't do any of the poses. But I sorta like spending time with Cam.

Who am I writing that to? It's not like anyone is reading this but me. This is exactly how it feels when Grams asks me to pray over dinner. I feel like I'm saying all this stuff that is bouncing back at me off the ceiling and landing in the spinach salad.

Cam probably didn't have to read my mind about wanting a journal at all. He's really smart. His early acceptance letter to this great college up north came last week. He's going to be a biochem major, which just makes me want to lie down on the floor and curl up in a ball. He's a brainiac. And on top of it he's nice and enthusiastic—which has a tendency to be dangerous.

Last semester Mom was always telling me to ask Cam for help with my geometry homework. I did, but instead of telling me what to do, Cam always talks and talks and talks. It's like he knows so much about stuff and likes math so much that he has to say it all instead of just the answer.

I stopped asking questions. It sort of annoyed me. Just did it myself, and didn't really understand it. I got a C in geometry. You'd have thought I'd flown a plane into a building. (That's bad to say, I guess. I mean, I know people died and everything, but it was a really long time ago.)

Dad came unglued. He's the chairman of the music department at the college where he works. He made me sign up for tutoring this summer with a student that his friend in the math department recommended. Our session starts in a few minutes. I was relieved when Nathan showed up the first time. I was afraid I'd get stuck with some weird math girl.

Nathan is a freshman. He's from Nebraska and has brown hair that's cut short. He works out a lot, and he wears these polo shirts with sleeves that are tight right around his biceps. I just stare at his arms a lot instead of listening when he's trying to help me find the answer.

I wish somebody would just tell me the answer.

Nathan's here. Gotta go.

Later . . .

OMG.

I TOTALLY JUST INVITED NATHAN TO MY BIRTHDAY DINNER.

OMG OMG OMG OMG

And

He

Said

YES!

This is totally crazy. I can't believe I actually said the words out loud. I didn't mean to. We were just sitting at the dining room table and he was talking about the hypotenuse of a right angle, and while he was looking at the protractor he was using to draw lines, I was staring at the lines of his jaw and noticed that they were almost a right angle, and the hypotenuse of the right angle of his jaw was this line in his cheek with a dimple in the middle that he gets when he smiles, and then I heard myself saying, You should come to my birthday dinner on Saturday, and then I realized that Mom was looking RIGHT AT ME like my hair was on fire, and I realized that I'd just invited an 18-year-old over for dinner in FRONT OF MY MOTHER. OMG. I just wanted to CRAWL UNDER THE TABLE.

But he stopped with his pencil stuck into the protractor and looked up, and then glanced over at Mom like he was looking to see if she'd heard, and she smiled at him, sort of weakly. I guess he took that to mean that it was okay with her 'cause he looked me right in the eye and said, Sure. That'd be fun. Now look at this triangle.

I tried to look at the triangle for the rest of the half hour, but I have no idea what he was saying. When he left, I walked him to the door, and Mom said, Nathan, come by around 7:30. He said, Sure thing, and you can call me Nate. He waved at me before he got in his pickup truck and said, See you this weekend. Then, he drove away. Just like that.

I went running back up to my bedroom and buried my head in my pillow and did one of those silent screams where you just breathe out really hard, but with no sound; it's sort of a soft roar, but the excitement on the inside of me made it feel like my head would explode.

I could hear my heart pounding in my ears, and I took a couple of deep breaths and then I remembered what Marty said in yoga this morning about trying to meditate and how to focus on the breath, so I sat down on the floor and crossed my legs like Marty does in front of class, and I closed my eyes and took really deep breaths and tried not to think about Nate. I could do it for about 5 breaths at a time, but then I'd see that line with the dimple in it behind my eyelids, and then the rest of his right-angle jaw would appear and I'd see a triangle fill in the space on his face.

I mean, it's really no big deal. My dad is two years older than my mom. Nate's only 18, and I'm 16, and it's not like he would be robbing the cradle or anything.

I think I really like him.

OMG I CAN'T BELIEVE THAT NATE IS COMING TO DINNER ON SATURDAY.

July 8

I was just standing in my mirror trying on a couple of different options for tonight. I passed my driver's test and got my license yesterday (YAY! OMG. Finally!), then Dad and I went shopping on the Promenade. I'm a really good bargain shopper. Cam worked at the Gap last summer and taught me to never EVER pay full-price for anything 'cause they just mark it down every two weeks. Primary, secondary, clearance. Primary, secondary, clearance. Every week on Tuesday night the markdowns would come through from the home office, and we'd all run around with those price-tag guns the next morning, marking down tops that some poor dope had paid $20 more for 12 hours ago. So, anyway, I got a lot of great stuff. Even Dad was surprised with how many items I got for $100. Well, then I splurged a little and added $40 from my savings to get these supercute sandals that I'd been wanting.

Anyway, I have all this stuff to try on, and I felt myself doing that thing I do where I put on, like, 12 different outfits and stand there and pick every single one of them apart, and I end up standing in front of the mirror in my underwear with this pile of really cute clothes with the tags still on them lying on the floor. I had just put on the second skirt I bought and could tell I was about to find something wrong with it, and then I just stopped, looked at myself, and thought: Don't be that girl.

I just don't want to be that chick who is always staring at herself in the mirror whining about how she looks and having a meltdown in the fitting room. I mean, I'm not a model or anything, but I think I look okay. I have already showered and straightened my hair. It's not frizzy or even curly really—just has some waves, and when you live this close to the waves it can get wavy. (God. Stupid joke.) Whatever, I stepped away from the mirror and saw my journal sitting on my desk, and I thought I'd write about it. I mean, this is a feeling. I'm not sure what kinds of feelings I'm supposed to be writing about in here, but maybe this is what crazy Marty the bird lady was talking about.

I'm SO EXCITED about Nate coming over and I want to look really hot, but the excitement also feels like nervousness, like I'm going to barf or something. Mom is downstairs putting a marinade on some shrimp that she's going to have Dad grill, and the smell when I walked through the kitchen made me feel like I was going to hurl up my toenails—and I LOVE shrimp.

I know I look good in this skirt. Dad told me it looked "far out" when I came out of the dressing room to check it out in the mirror. He said this in his I'm-being-a-little-too-loud-so-the-other-people-present-will-hear-me-and-think-I'm-hilarious-when-really-I'm-just-torturing-my-daughter voice. I told him to please be quiet and offer his opinions only regarding possible escape routes in the case of a fire, or a random stampede of wild bison. In all other matters, I respectfully asked him to please refrain from speaking to me until we had reached the cash wrap.

I looked in the mirror again just now. This skirt totally works.

Weird how excited and scared feel like the same thing.

July 8—11:30 p.m.

I shoulda known.

I shoulda known when he walked up the front steps with flowers and handed them to Mom.

But he brought me a card with a joke about having pi on my birthday instead of cake (guh-rooooan) and it had a $25 gift card for iTunes in it. Which was cool and so sweet of him, but he just signed his name. Shoulda known when he didn't

10

write anything personal. Just "Happy B-Day! Nate."

But he was really funny and sweet at dinner. He sat across from me and told us all this hilarious story about when he was growing up in Nebraska and he and his brother raised sheep for the county fair. (Yes. Apparently people still raise animals and take them to fairs where they win ribbons and titles and scholarships. Thank you, CHARLOTTE'S WEB.)

One morning he and his brother went out to scoop food out of these big 25-pound sacks of feed for the sheep, and there was a mouse in one of the bags that ran up his little brother's jacket sleeve. He was telling us about how he thought his brother had been possessed by a demon because he kept screaming and shaking his arms and beating at his chest and running around in a circle while the mouse wriggled around inside his shirt. We were all crying, we were laughing so hard, and Cam almost inhaled a bite of shrimp, which sent him on a coughing fit that made the rest of us laugh even harder.

He jumped up and helped me clear the table when Mom asked who wanted dessert. When Mom told him he didn't need to do that, he smiled at me and said, Oh yes, ma'am, I do. My mama'd fly in from Grand Island and smack me if I didn't.

When we were in the kitchen, I started rinsing plates and he loaded them into the dishwasher like he lived here. We were laughing and joking around and no one mentioned geometry.

He was so easy to talk to, easy to be near. I didn't feel nervous even once. I couldn't help but wonder what it would feel like if we were married and this was our house and we were loading the dishwasher together. That's probably stupid, but it made me feel hopeful inside, like maybe something like that was possible.

When Nate bent over to put the final plate in the dishwasher, a necklace fell out of his shirt. It had a tiny key on it, and I was about to ask him where he got it, but Mom came into the kitchen to get some coffee mugs and the French press. Nate tucked the necklace back into his polo before I could ask him about it, but I shoulda known.

There's a long porch on the back of our house that looks over the bottom of the canyon out to the water. We ate dessert out there. Dad lit the candles in the big lanterns on the table outside. Cam sat next to Nate and they talked soccer. The flicker made their skin glow like they were on the beach at sunset. Nate looked all sun-kissed and happy. I felt a foot nudge mine just for a second under the table and my heart started racing. I was glad that it was just the candles outside in the dark 'cause I started to blush like crazy. I thought maybe Nate had touched my foot, and I kept sliding mine a little bit closer toward him under the table, but his foot never touched mine again.

It was almost 10 when he pulled out his phone and checked it, then said, Whoa. I gotta go.

I felt really bummed all of a sudden, and then silly. What was I hoping? That he'd stay and walk me down to the beach? He stood up and shook my dad's hand, then gave Cam one of those weird hugs that guys give each other where they grab hands like they're gonna shake and then lean in and hug with their arms caught in between them. He kissed my mom on the cheek and told her what a good cook she was.

Then he looked right at me and said, Will you walk me to my truck?

I got so many butterflies in my stomach, I thought they might start flying out of my ears. I said SURE, and realized that nobody had really heard him ask that because Mom was pouring more wine and Dad was pouring more coffee and Cam was texting somebody. So I slipped into the house and out the front door.

He'd parked on the street, and when he got to the door of his pickup, he leaned against it and looked up at the sky and said, Huh.

I said, What?

He told me that in Nebraska at this time of night you could see lots of stars. I followed his gaze up to the sky, but I knew there wouldn't be any stars. Out here, the sky just glows this weird purply color even on the darkest night here. It's the light pollution bouncing off of the marine layer, I said. It's what

13

happens at night when 8 million people get jammed up against the ocean. I turned around and stood next to him with my back up against the truck.

He said it was funny how you always hear about all the stars in Los Angeles, but at night in Nebraska, it's like the sky is covered with diamonds. Then he looked over at me, and I don't know what happened, but I just knew that I had to feel his lips on mine. So I leaned in and kissed him.

Nate jumped like I'd shot him with a taser. He said, WHOA, what are you doing? OMG! I was SO EMBARRASSED I couldn't even LOOK at him. It was like we were having this PERFECT night, and then BLAM-O: I broke the spell. I was blushing and stammering and then I felt the tears come to my eyes, and I didn't wait. I just sprinted back across the street toward the house. I was not going to let him see me cry.

As my foot hit the curb on the other side of the street, he said WAIT!

There was something in the way he said it that made me turn around. And then he shook his head and smacked his forehead, and he walked over to me, and just looked at me. He pushed my hair over my shoulder and said, No. I'm sorry.

He told me that I had come along two years too late. And that I was beautiful. And that he has a girlfriend.

I shoulda thought about that. I shoulda never invited him to dinner tonight.

I shoulda known.

July 10

Thank GOD I don't have a session with Nate this week 'cause of the midterm. I would never date a guy who drives a stupid pickup truck.

ALSO? He's a total liar. I am plenty of things, but I am not beautiful.

July 13

Took the geometry midterm in summer school today. I think I did okay. We don't have class again until Monday. Only 4 more weeks to go, then I finally get a stupid month off.

[Sad trombone . . .]

July 14

Cam and I got to go to the 1 p.m. yoga class today because I didn't have geometry. Usually I am in class until noon, and it's too rushed to go to Marty's 1 p.m. class, so we go to the 3 p.m. class. Of course, Cam always gets up early to run so that he stays in shape for soccer. Practices start way before school does and he always says that the only thing that sucks worse than two-a-days in July is two-a-days in July when you didn't run in June.

There's a whole different crowd at Marty's 1 p.m. class. I was not expecting that. It totally changes the feeling in the room. This class had more guys in it and a crazy lady who musta been like 45 years old who was wearing only her bra and some bicycle shorts—and not like a sports bra. She was wearing just a regular old ivory-colored bra. Lace on the cups. Underwire. In yoga. Like it was no big deal. I wanted to pull her aside and be like, um, okay. I know you probably don't understand that there's a difference between a regular bra and a sports bra because they cover about the same amount of skin and all that BUT. THERE. IS.

Siiiiiiiiiiiiiiiiiiiiiiiiiiiiiiiiiiiiiiiiiiiiiiigh.

July 15

I almost didn't go back to the 1 p.m. class with Cam today.

I'm really glad I did, though. And I know how this is going to sound before I even write it down, but fine: YES. It's because of a boy. There. I said it. I'm becoming one of those starry-eyed, dewey-cheeked bimbos. I can't help it.

I was staring at Crazy Bra Lady (today's bra was black) while we were doing side planks and I noticed this guy watching me watch her in the mirror. He was about my age and had longish brown hair that was kinda shaggy, but cool shaggy not gross shaggy, and he was really tan. When I saw him looking at me, he got this little smile, like he knew a secret about me.

After class, Cam went into the bathroom to change shorts and I was waiting outside on the sidewalk, watching Crazy Bra Lady unlock her bike. She'd put on a big T-shirt that had the neck cut out of it so it hung off one shoulder. As I watched her pedal away, I heard this voice behind me say, She is totally wackadoodle.

When I turned around, it was shaggy brown hair guy who flipped his bangs out of his eyes and said, Hey, I'm Ross.

I told him my name, and he got that little smile again. I said, What? Do you know something I don't know? And he was like, Maybe.

I said, You gonna keep it a secret?

He grinned at me and said he was just hoping I'd be back. He said, I saw you yesterday but you and your boyfriend left before I could say hi.

I frowned at him and said, My boyfriend? right as Cam walked out the front door with his yoga mat slung over his shoulder and said, You have a boyfriend?

Ross frowned and said, Oh. Then . . . who are you?

Cam frowned and said, Who are YOU?

Finally I pointed at Cam and said BROTHER, then pointed at Ross and said ROSS.

Boys are so weird.

Cam and Ross shook hands and then we went to get
smoothies and Cam gave Ross the third degree during which
we learned:

1. Cam should play a detective on CSI.

2. Ross is 16 years old like me.

3. Ross just moved here from Florida.

4. Ross's mom got a job as an associate events
manager at this big resort hotel on the beach.

5. Ross can go hang out at the pool at the
hotel when his mom is working.

6. Ross has A-MA-ZING blue eyes.

Cam probably learned more, but when I noticed the eyes,
I sorta stopped listening. As we walked back to our cars, Ross
invited us to come to the hotel for a swim later, but Cam was
headed to the beach, and I promised Mom that I'd vacuum
and dust today 'cause I didn't do it on Saturday because it was

my birthday (observed), and then I was sorta glum on Sunday. I think she knew it was something about Nate even though I didn't tell her about it.

Ross stopped in front of a pickup truck and I thought Holy. Hell. What is it with guys and pickup trucks??? But I just said, You drive a pickup? And he said, How else am I gonna haul my surfboard around? and all of a sudden, Ross was 27-times cuter than I already thought he was.

Then he said, I'm gonna paddle out tomorrow morning sorta early. Wanna come? We can hang out on the beach after I catch a couple waves.

I glanced at Cam, who punched Ross in the shoulder and said, Dude. You can't ask my sister out with me standing right here.

And I was like OMG CAM! SHUT UP.

And Ross got his little secret smile again, and Cam cracked up while Ross tapped my number into his phone.

He's coming by to pick me up at 7 a.m. tomorrow.

I have to go dust and vacuum now.

I AM SO EXCITED. HE'S SO CUTE.

Later . . .

I told Mom and Dad about Ross over dinner. They were all, We've never met this young man. We don't want you running around with kids we haven't met.

ARRRRRRRRGH. They're soooooooooooo uptight sometimes.

But Cam came to the rescue and vouched for Ross, and they finally agreed to let me go on the condition that they get to meet him first.

I texted Ross after dinner: My parents want to meet you in the AM b4 we go.

He wrote back right away: KEWL. C U AT 7 =)

Now if I can just keep the chitchat to a minimum tomorrow morning we'll be set.

Later . . .

Maybe I was wrong about guys with pickup trucks. Guess it depends on the guy.

July 16

I am writing this on the beach. I packed my journal and a pen in the bag with my towel and a couple of magazines, a bottle of water, and some sunscreen. I set my alarm for 6 a.m. so that I would be up early enough to take a shower and put on some waterproof mascara. I didn't want to look like I'd just crawled out from under a rock when Ross got here.

He rolled up right at 7 a.m. on the dot, amazingly punctual for a surfer. He was wearing a hoodie and a cap, and I could see the surfboard sticking out of his pickup truck in the driveway. I don't know if it was the fact that it was so early in the morning or what, but Mom and Dad were both really well-behaved. Mom smiled and was friendly; Dad didn't make any jokes that only he thinks are funny.

As we climbed into the truck, I was nervous that my brain wouldn't really work right as far as coming up with things to say. Ross was sort of quiet at first, and I felt that nervous feeling in my stomach like somebody was tap dancing in my rib cage. As we drove up the highway along the coast, Ross kept eyeing the water, like he had forgotten I was there. I felt my face get flushed, and I felt out of place, and then I felt embarrassed, and then I felt . . . ANGRY.

I did NOT shave my legs and put on waterproof mascara before dawn to be IGNORED.

Almost, as if he could read my thoughts, Ross flipped his bangs out of his eyes and said, This part always makes me nervous.

I laughed, and said, ME TOO! I said it a little too loudly and with a little too much enthusiasm, but he smiled over at me and said, Yeah! I know, right? It's always like will there be good waves or not??? And I realized that we were talking about two completely different things. He wasn't talking about being alone in the truck with me for the first time and figuring

21

out what to say. He was checking the coastline for waves.

I thought briefly about just opening the door and throwing myself out of the truck, but just as I was trying to gauge how soft the tall grass along the shoulder might be and whether I would clear the concrete and gravel part, Ross must've found what he was looking for and pulled off the road. I recognized this part of the coast. It's the place where the beach line dips in toward the highway and creates a little bay with a natural surf break. Ross eased his truck off the road and parallel parked between two other cars on the side of the highway.

He was all business, and I could tell he wanted to be in the water ASAP. He jumped out of the truck, pointed at the water, and whooped something that sounded like "hella goody nugs." Then he raced around to the back of his truck and pulled off his cap and hoodie and T-shirt all in one swift movement.

And I forgot that I was mad.

And I forgot that he hadn't looked at me twice.

And I forgot that he hadn't probably given a second thought to how smooth my legs were.

All I could see were his p-e-r-f-e-c-t chest and his ABS. OMG.

Ross.

Has.

Some.

ABS.

He wrapped a towel around his waist and traded his board shorts for a wet suit that was in the bed of his truck under his board. I'd always seen surfers with their wet suits peeled down on the one hundred zillion other times I've driven by this surf break. (Hey! Look! I sound like I know what I'm talking about!) I always just thought that they unzipped the back and pulled down the top part because they were hot. I didn't know that they were in the process of GETTING NAKED IN BROAD DAYLIGHT under a TOWEL!

I'm not even sure how he did it so fast, but about 30 seconds after we parked, we were picking our way down the path toward the beach. Well, Ross was like scampering down, balancing a board and pulling up his wet suit and using words I didn't really completely understand to describe the waves.

He's surfing right now. I can sometimes make out which one is him. There are about 10 people out there trying to catch a wave. One of them is a girl with blond braids. Sometimes I think it would be fun to surf, but the water is so cold that it makes me shiver just to think about it. The sun is already trying to break through the marine layer, and I hope that it will so I can take off my hoodie and T-shirt and get some sun. I have a really cute swimsuit on underneath my shorts.

I wonder if Ross will think I look sexy?

I've never really done anything with a boy except kiss.

OMG! Ross just caught a huge wave and rode it all the way in!

July 16, 2 p.m.

I just got back from the beach with Ross, and I can't believe what happened. He offered me drugs. I'm not even sure I should write those words down. I mean, what if my MOM FINDS THIS??? It's so weird. I had such a good time sitting on the beach watching Ross surf, and after a couple of hours he came and sat with me. He unzipped his wet suit and pulled it down halfway. He has those little V lines that plunged into his wet suit from his abs, and I had to concentrate so that I didn't just stare at them the whole time.

We talked for a while. Or, well, I talked. A lot. More than I usually do. Ross just kept asking me about my family, and growing up here and what it was like. He kept telling me that I have a really pretty smile. Like a movie star, he said. He laughed and called me Hollywood. It's funny. Now that I think about it, I didn't really ask him any questions at all. I felt so excited the whole time that he seemed to want to know all about me, and he just kept asking me questions.

THEN!

We headed back up to his truck, and after he slid his surfboard into the back, he shimmied out of his wetsuit using that little towel trick again. Some girls drove by in a silver BMW while he was pulling his suit out from under the towel and honked and screamed out the window. At first it made me blush, but then I thought how cool it was that I was the girl with the guy that other girls were honking at.

When we got into his truck, Ross popped open the console on the armrest between us and pulled out a little glass pipe and a lighter. He brought the pipe to his lips, sparked the lighter over the bowl, then sucked air in, causing the flame to dip into the bowl. A little cloud of white smoke floated up from the glowing embers in the pipe, and Ross held the smoke in his lungs for a second before rolling down his window a couple inches and exhaling out the crack at the top.

This weird, sweet, stinky smell filled the cab of the truck, and I knew that it was weed, but I have never smelled it that strong before. I was afraid my hair would smell like it.

I've seen people smoke pot in movies and on TV, but I've NEVER seen anybody do it in real life. I mean, I think Cam smokes pot. I've heard him and his friends joke around about it, but he's not like a stoner or anything. I felt my heart sort of speed up while I watched Ross smoke, then he turned to me and held the pipe toward me.

He asked me if I wanted a hit.

NO!

I said it fast like I was scared someone might be listening. I was just A. MAZED. that he even thought I looked like a girl who smoked pot. Then I was really worried that he would be mad at me that I didn't want any. I felt like I had answered too fast. I didn't want him to think that I didn't like him just because he smoked pot. What if he didn't like me now?

I shouldn't have worried. He just laughed and said he figured I was a straight edge but that you couldn't blame a boy for trying.

My cheeks are red again now just writing this down. I have to make sure Mom doesn't find this journal and think it's my schoolwork. Not that she'd actually read my journal on purpose; at least I don't think she would. Anyway, I'm going to hide it under some other stuff on my desk, just in case.

I like Ross. I don't want Mom not to let me hang out with him just 'cause he smokes pot.

Ross invited me to come over to the hotel where his mom works tomorrow after yoga and lie out at the pool with him.

Oh yeah, and when we were lying on the beach talking, he told me my suit was "cute." I think he really likes me.

July 17

CAM IS TAKING ME TO MY FIRST BIG PARTY!!!!!!!!!!
    IT'S ON SATURDAAAAAAAAAAAAAAY!!!!!!!!!!!!!!!!!
    THAT'S TOMORROOOOOOOOOOOOOOW!!!!!!!!!!!

I CAN'T WAAAAAAAAAAAAAAAAAAAIT!!!!!!!!!!!!!!!!

I can't believe he said yes. I heard him talking to his friend Jason about it, and he was like, If Elizabeth Archer's sister is going to be there, I'm THERE.

Elizabeth Archer is this blond cheerleader in my class at school, and she's really pretty, and really nice, but is dumb as a stump. Her older sister is a freshman in college this year, and is just as pretty, only she has red hair and was valedictorian last year. She speaks French and Spanish fluently and is on track to finish her undergrad degree in 3 years. Cam has followed her around like a drooling puppy since he was in 9th grade and she was a sophomore.

I heard him hang up with Jason and go YES! really loudly, and that's when I wandered into his room and said, If Elizabeth Archer is going, can I go?

He opened his mouth to say NO like he always does, but then he looked up at me and really saw me. He sat and sort of looked at me for a minute, like he was taking me in, and then he smiled, and said, Why not?

I jumped up and down and screamed like a moron on a game show, and he laughed and said, But only if you stop screaming right now and promise never to do that again.

I immediately shut up and said, I promise I won't get in your way.

And then Cam said the nicest thing to me. He said, You're not in the way, sis. I like hanging with you.

Which is weird 'cause usually brothers and sisters our age don't always get along, but I realized that Cam is maybe the best brother in the whole galaxy.

July 19

Last night was the party and it was really awful and really great all at the same time. God, sometimes I write stuff down in this journal that just doesn't make any sense at all. If anyone ever finds this, they'll have me committed for being a crazy person.

I'm not sure how I feel about last night. I still can't believe how it all went down. The only two things I know for sure are:

1. Pot is GREAT.
2. Ross is AMAZING.

Cam drove us to Jason's place with strict instructions from Mom and Dad to keep an eye on me. Jason's house was already pretty crowded when we got there and Cam steered us through the living room to the kitchen where he gave Jason a high five and I saw Elizabeth Archer talking to this guy with shaggy brown hair who looked a lot like . . . ROSS!

It was totally him, and I felt my stomach drop like I was on a roller coaster. I couldn't believe he was here too. Elizabeth saw me and waved, and Ross turned around and got this big goofy smile on his face like he was really happy to see me. He came over to say hi to me and Cam and grabbed a couple of beers out of a cooler on his way around the island in Jason's giant kitchen. He handed one to Cam and then held one out to me.

I felt my cheeks go hot, and I glanced up at Cam like, Should I do this? Is this okay?

He laughed and said, You won't like it, sis.

Well, I wasn't about to let Cam tell me what to do for the whole night, so I grabbed the beer and took a big swig. It was cold and bubbly like soda, but as I swallowed it, the taste turned sour and sweet in a really weird way that made me start to gag a little, and I made a face that must've been really funny and a noise that felt like I was trying not to throw up, sort of an URGGGH sound, and Cam and Jason laughed as I handed the beer back to Ross.

Cam was right again. He's right about everything. Beer tastes pretty gross.

Ross got a phone call and held up a finger as he answered and disappeared around a corner toward the front door. Cam saw Megan Archer out by the pool and grabbed Jason and pushed him toward the glass doors that led out back. My face was still pretty red from the beer and the embarrassment. I was really worried that Ross thought I was a moron now. Elizabeth patted my back and smiled her big loopy smile. She said, I hate beer too. Let's get some wine coolers.

I told her I was okay and just wanted to go get some fresh air. She thought this was a good idea and grabbed a bright red bottle of something out of one of the coolers, then took my hand and dragged me out toward the pool and over to the fire pit.

Jason and Cam were over at the hot tub talking to Megan, and Elizabeth and I sat down by this girl I'd never seen before. She was sipping a wine cooler too, and she smiled at us as we sat down.

Elizabeth introduced herself, and the girl told us her name was Astrid. Elizabeth asked her what school she went to, and she told us she was transferring to our school for her senior year. Apparently, she was sick of the Catholic school she'd been attending and convinced her dad to let her go to public school for her last year. She'd come to the party with her boyfriend, who knew Megan and was getting a drink.

I sat there feeling sort of invisible. I wasn't nearly as pretty as Elizabeth or Astrid or Megan, and I couldn't shake the feeling that everybody at this party was older and cooler than I was. I mean, I know that Elizabeth is my age and not very smart where school is concerned, but she's so pretty, I sort of felt like I could have disappeared and no one would have noticed. I felt like a dweeb who couldn't even keep down a swallow of beer.

I wanted to go find Ross and hang out with him, but I was still feeling like I'd disappointed him somehow by not liking the beer he brought me. Maybe he was hanging out with other girls. Girls who drink beer. I was thinking about all of the ways that Ross probably thought I was lame when Astrid noticed I wasn't drinking anything and offered me her wine cooler.

She smiled and asked if I wanted to try some. She said, You look like you're not having a very good time. This will help.

And right at that moment, I DID want to try some. I DID want to have a good time. I just didn't want to be that quiet girl in the corner not talking to anybody at the party.

So I said YES.

The wine cooler was cold and not as bubbly as the beer. It was really really really SWEET. Like, too sweet. It felt like I was drinking snow-cone syrup straight from the bottle. But it was better than beer. At least this was fruity. I couldn't tell if it was strawberry or watermelon or cherry. It just tasted . . . red.

I smiled at Astrid and said thanks. She laughed and said no problem. Elizabeth jumped up and went into the kitchen to get more wine coolers and brought them back. I couldn't really tell any difference in how I felt. I've never been drunk, but I sort of felt . . . lighter somehow. I think it was probably because I didn't feel so lame. These girls were cool and pretty and they were sitting here talking to me like I was one of them, like I belonged there.

I took a drink of the new wine cooler that Elizabeth handed me, and then we were talking about the boys we thought were cute. Elizabeth asked me how I knew Ross, and I told her and Astrid all about meeting Ross at yoga and how we'd gone to the beach together. All of a sudden, as I was talking, I let out a little burp from the wine cooler and my eyes got wide and I slapped a hand over my mouth and started giggling.

Astrid and Elizabeth laughed really hard too, and it felt so good to share a funny moment with these girls who I barely knew. I felt my stomach turn a little bit, and I realized I hadn't eaten much dinner because I was nervous about going to the party. These wine coolers had a lot of sugar in them and maybe it was that or the alcohol that was making my stomach hurt. I told Astrid my stomach felt kind of weird, and she smiled and rubbed her hand on my back. She told me not to worry. You'll get the hang of it, she said, and nodded at the wine cooler. Maybe have a glass of water after that one before you have more. You know, pace yourself.

Then Astrid looked up as she saw a guy walk through the glass doors and come out onto the pool deck. She jumped up and said, Oh, there's my boyfriend. I'm gonna go say hi. See you two later. I watched as she picked her way through the crowd around the pool toward the stairs at the door. She walked up behind this muscular guy on the stairs and put her arms around his waist.

When he turned around, I gasped really loudly and Elizabeth looked at me and said, What?

It was Nathan.

Astrid was Nathan's girlfriend.

Now I really felt sick to my stomach and a little dizzy. I stood up quickly, and all of a sudden I felt the wine cooler hit me, and I sat back down really fast 'cause I thought I might fall down. I closed my eyes and turned away from Nate and Astrid. I didn't want him to see me. I didn't want him to know I was here. I leaned back into the shadows from the hedge at the back of the concrete bench that was carved around the fire pit.

Elizabeth was like, Do you know him?

I nodded. I told her he was my geometry tutor, but even as I said it, I wished I'd kept that to myself.

Elizabeth turned back to watch as Nate and Astrid walked over to join Megan, Cam, and Jason in the hot tub. I put down my wine cooler and stepped over Elizabeth Archer and all of her questions and ran into the house.

I had to find Ross.

When I didn't see him in the kitchen, I headed into the

living room and almost ran into him head-on. He started to say that he'd been looking for me, but I guess the look on my face made him stop short. He asked me if I was okay, and suddenly my eyes filled up with tears and I felt even more like a COMPLETE IDIOT. Oh. My. GOD. I was about to start crying in the middle of my first party, and Ross was completely cool. He looked over both shoulders, then grabbed my elbow and steered me across the living room and up the stairs in the entryway so fast it made me a little dizzy.

I followed Ross into the master bedroom, and he pushed out two French doors onto a balcony that overlooked the backyard. I could see the hot tub and fire pit on opposite sides of the pool. I stood at the rail and looked out at the shadows silhouetted by the flames of the fire pit and the lights under the water in the hot tub. I couldn't make out his face, but I knew Nate was out there. With Astrid.

Ross joined me at the rail and said, So. How's my straight edge?

I felt his arm against mine. It was warm, and he followed my gaze down toward the hot tub. I told him I wasn't such a straight edge tonight.

He laughed and said, Nah, you're just ON edge.

He nodded toward the hot tub and asked who I was looking at. It came pouring out. We plopped down on the patio furniture and I told him all about Nate and the night I tried to kiss him, and about Astrid and the wine coolers. As he listened, Ross pulled a joint out of his pocket and lit it. He took several drags and then held it out to me. I couldn't believe it, but I just took it from him. I told myself it was because I'd already drunk a wine cooler, but really it was because I just didn't want to feel like a loser. Ross is so cool and handsome. I want to feel like a really hot girl. I want Ross to want me the way Cam wants Megan Archer.

I put the joint to my lips, and Ross told me to suck slowly on the end and take a deep breath. I could taste the smoke as it rolled into my mouth over my tongue, then I sort of squinted and inhaled it in a quick deep breath. It tickled the back of my throat so bad that I started coughing really hard. I must've dragged in more smoke than I thought because I could see it puff out around me, even in the dark.

Ross tossed his bangs out of his eyes while he took another long, deep drag off of the joint. I watched the way he held the smoke in for a long time before he blew it out. He cut his eyes my direction with a little smirk and asked, Wanna try again?

I smiled back at him and took the joint. This time I was more prepared. I sucked in very slowly, and the tickle at the back of my throat wasn't quite as bad. Then I held the smoke in my lungs for as long as I could, and when I blew it out, I only coughed once.

Ross whistled and laughed. Dang, girl, he said. That's a big hit. You're gonna feel fine in about 5 minutes.

We settled back on the little patio love seat and kicked our feet up on the bench in front of us. He laid his head on my shoulder, and we looked up at the moon over the palm trees. For a second we were real quiet, and then he put his hand on my leg and said, Sorry about the thing with Nate. I shrugged, and my heart was beating really fast, and after a couple more minutes I started singing along with this song that was blasting out of the speakers by the pool. Then I started laughing, and Ross started laughing too. Uh-oh, he said. And I was like What? And he said, Somebody is stoned!

And then I realized that I felt good! Really good! Deep down to my feet good! I didn't even care about stupid Nate and Astrid anymore. I could sort of feel a weird floating feeling in my brain, like it was all calm and cool in there, and my toes were a little buzzy somehow, and all of a sudden I wanted a drink, something cool and bubbly and NOT a wine cooler.

Ross musta had the same thought 'cause right at that second he said, Let's get outta here, and I said, I want french fries, and he laughed like that was the funniest thing he'd ever heard.

He grabbed me and said, Of course you do. Damn. You're hilarious.

I followed Ross downstairs and waited in the kitchen while

he ran out to the hot tub to tell Cam he was going to take me to get some food and then home. Then we jumped into his truck and headed over to Swingers, where I had the biggest plate of french fries I've ever seen and I didn't give a crap about the calories because they tasted so good. We went through three sides of ranch and half a bottle of ketchup and we sat on the same side of the booth with our feet up on the other side.

The thing that makes Ross so different from other boys is that he listens. He just listened to me talk blah blah blah blah blah for like hours about Nate. And he just kept eating french fries. And ordering chocolate malts. And dipping french fries into the chocolate malts.

And then I felt all weird and spacey in my head, like maybe I'd been talking for at least 23 years without shutting up, and I was really thirsty, and I got worried. I was worried that Ross was bored and that he wasn't having a good time and that I was being one of those whiny girls who complains about everything all the time to everyone and turns everyone off. So I took a really long drink of my Diet Coke through a straw, and just as I was about to turn to Ross and ask if he was totally bored, I felt him lean over and kiss me on the cheek.

Then he laid his head on my shoulder and said, I get it.

We just sat there in the booth for a long time, and I felt his head on my shoulder and I stopped being worried. I got this really happy feeling, like this floaty place in my chest because I knew that Ross did get it. He didn't have to say another word.

We're going to the beach tomorrow.

I can't wait.

July 20

I just got back from the beach with Ross. We smoked another joint before we got out of his truck. It was so much fun! I feel like smoking pot used to be this thing that I was like TOTALLY AGAINST because of all the stuff that everybody tells you and because of the people who you see at school who do it. They're all like fuzz heads who need to clean their fingernails. But Ross is different. And now I'm different. Probably because I'm making the decision to do what I want. I never realized how much I let everyone else decide what I'm going to do. I mean, we started having policemen come to school in what—like 3rd grade?—to tell us that pot is so eeeeeeeeeeevil and WRONG. But, actually, I've smoked two joints now and I'm still going to my geometry class in summer school. No big deal.

Anyway, the beach was good. It was nice to lie in the sun while Ross surfed, and then he sat on the beach with me and we talked. Or, actually, I talked. I'm always the one talking. It was weird at the end. I asked him some questions about Florida and the move out here and the school he went to and his friends there. He didn't really talk about it. Just said that his dad was an asshole and that he was glad his mom got this job. And then he checked his phone and was like, We have to go, and he seemed to be in a really big hurry.

It kind of pissed me off. Totally ruined that floaty feeling I was having from the joint. I feel like he wanted to go hang out with someone else and he didn't want me there. I wish I had my own joint right this very second.

July 22

Tried texting Ross after summer school today, but I never heard back. It's weird. When we're together, he feels like my best friend, and then he just disappears. I wonder what it'd be like to hold his hand? I want to try to when we go to the beach the next time. Maybe when we're walking up to his truck. But he's always holding that damn surfboard. I really want him to text me back. Dad and Mom were all over me tonight about how geometry is going and I know they really care, it's just that I don't know how it's going. I mean, I guess fine. I passed the midterm. Got a B. No big whoop.

ROSS, TEXT ME BACK.

July 25

Oh. My. Gosh.

Just got back from hanging out with Ross and Cam at

the hotel where Ross's mom works. This morning Ross
F-I-N-A-L-L-Y texted me back. He told me that Cam and
I should bring our swimsuits and meet him at this new yoga
class this afternoon. It's at the place where we usually go, but
earlier. Luckily Cam had the day off from cleaning pools, so he
came and got me at school and we went to meet Ross.

When I asked him if he got my texts yesterday, all he said
was, Yeah. Sorry. I was busy.

I was like WHAT. EVER. But it was still really good to
see him. Ugh! Sometimes I'm so like one of those dippy girls
I just HATE who are like all gross over some guy who treats
them like crap. I mean, not that Ross is treating me like crap.
Maybe he WAS busy. Maybe it's something weird with his dad
or something. I don't know. ARGH. SEE? THIS is why I need
to smoke a joint sometime! My head just goes on this giant
Tilt-A-Whirl and I can't make it stop.

ANY

WAY

We got to this new class and there was this teacher named
Ian who Ross knows. Ian is a sophomore at the college where
my Dad works, and he apparently teaches yoga on the side. Ross
met him at a party at the beach on Saturday. He's got blond
spiky hair and a friendly smile. He's a little too tan if you ask
me, but I guess he and Ross are surfing buddies or something.

There was a lot of "whassup" and "dude" and "bro," only it sounds like they're saying "bra" and general weird boy talk. Cam even got into it.

I wish I had a friend who is a girl to talk to like that. I mean, not LIKE that, but someone who I felt like I was close to. It was sort of instant with these guys.

Anyway, after class we were all talking while we headed over to the hotel, and Ross told us that Ian has a friend named Blake who has a beach house up the coast. Then he said that Blake was having a party this weekend, and almost before he finished the sentence, I was like YES I WANT TO GO TO THE PARTY! That made Ross and Cam crack up, and I thought about how perfect this summer was turning out to be because I had met Ross and Cam was treating me like an adult.

When we got to the hotel Ross's mom was in meetings or something, but the concierge told us "hi" and joked around with Ross and then let us go lie out by the pool. We went and changed clothes in the locker rooms by the pool where they had towels and everything. It was SO NICE.

But then Ross and Cam went into the bathroom together and I think they totally smoked pot because when they came out, they were sort of giggling. Ross started talking on and on about how cool Ian was and how much fun they had the other night at the party, and I realized THAT was the night I was texting him, so he wasn't busy with anything like his dad, just at a big party.

I got really quiet because I was feeling left out. I mean, it wasn't fair that Cam and Ross got to get stoned and I didn't, and it REALLY wasn't cool of Ross to not return my text messages when he was just at a party. I mean HOW HARD IS IT TO TEXT AT A PARTY??? GRRRR.

Then the boys got hungry and Ross ordered food that they brought out for us right there at the pool, and we didn't even have to pay for it. He said his mom got an expense account at the hotel every month for clients and it was okay with her if he got lunch for himself and friends as long as he didn't spend too much.

The food helped, because I realized I was really hungry from yoga, but then Ross noticed I was being superquiet and asked what was up.

I just said, Nothing, but he wouldn't let it go, so I told him. Well, I whispered it. I said:

I want a hit.

And Cam heard me and said, You won't really like it.

And I shot him a look and said, I already really like it. You don't know everything about me.

Cam frowned for a second, and then Ross busted out laughing like it was the funniest thing ever. When Cam heard that, he started laughing too. I said, See? You're both high as kites so everything is funny. NOT. FAIR.

Ross promised me that he would smoke me out at the party on Saturday.

Cam was laughing too, but he kept looking over at me and then looking away on the drive home. I hope he isn't getting all Big Brotherly on me.

July 26

I just got back from Cam's bedroom and I'm SHAKING. I can barely hold the pen to write this in the journal. Oh my God. My handwriting looks like crap.

I can't BELIEVE what just happened.

Cam has to work really early on Saturday morning cleaning a pool for these people who have this big party planned for their kids. He told me that he couldn't go to the party because he has to get in bed really early.

I told him that Ross could take me to the party, and he said, I don't feel comfortable with that.

I told him that I didn't care what he felt comfortable with, I was going to this party with Ross and Ian no matter what.

He just stared at me. I was standing in the doorway of his room, and he got up and pulled me in and closed the door. He was like, Do you want me to tell Mom and Dad that you've been running around smoking weed with Ross?

I just stared at him. I said, Are you serious? Because I'll march right in there this second and tell them that you've been smoking pot with Ross in PUBLIC. At the HOTEL. And who knows where else? And I'll also tell them that you were standing right there when I had my first beer.

I sort of wished I hadn't said that because he looked hurt, but I mean, come on! You're going to THREATEN me? He rolled his eyes and said, I can't believe you've been smoking pot.

I said, Look. I've had two puffs off of two different joints. It's not like I'm some crazy stoner chick. I just liked it. It's no big deal.

Finally I got him to agree that I could go and he wouldn't tell Mom and Dad anything.

I just got a text back from Ross. He and Ian are going to swing by and pick me up in 2 hours.

OMG.

WHAT AM I GOING TO WEAR???

Later . . .
Cam came into the bathroom while I was putting on my makeup and just leaned against the door. He was watching me in the mirror while I put on mascara, and he asked how I could do that

without poking my eye out. I told him I am talented. He cracked a smile for the first time all day. Finally.

Then he came over and hugged me and told me that I was pretty.

I laughed and told him to stop being a weirdo.

But really, it made me feel so good on the inside, like he finally accepts that I can make my own decisions, like he doesn't just see me as his stupid kid sister anymore.

Oh! He just called for me. Ian and Ross must be here. He's insisting on walking me out so that he can be all big brother and tell them to take good care of me.

July 27

Holy crap. HOLY CRAP!

I don't even know where to begin. My head is in 100 thousand different places. AND POUNDING LIKE A JACKHAMMER. This is the first time I've been able to sit up all morning, but I had to write all of this down so I don't forget!

First things first: So, Ross and Ian came in to meet Mom and Dad, because of course when they found out that Cam wasn't going to the party, Mom almost had a heart attack and wasn't going to let me go. Luckily Dad was cleaning up the flower bed out front when Ross and Ian pulled up, and he recognized Ian. Apparently Ian was in a section of music theory last fall that Dad teaches. He and Dad were laughing and talking when Mom stormed out to say that I couldn't go to the party, and Dad introduced her to Ian, and Ian was really charming and promised that they'd have me back home by midnight and that nothing bad would happen.

I HATE hearing people say that they'll "keep an eye on me." As if I'm some crazy person who might just EXPLODE at any moment. Whatever. Ian told Mom that he really loved her impatiens in the flower bed that Dad was weeding and how he used to work in a nursery. Then they talked for like 29 years about soil types, and Ross and Cam and I were almost comatose from boredom by the time Mom finally glanced over at me and said that it was okay if I went to the party.

So FINALLY we got in the car, and I was so happy to finally get out of there that I didn't even mind that Ross sat up front with Ian. I mean, I guess it would have been weird for him to sit in the back with me, but I thought that maybe he'd at least offer me the front seat. Whatever.

So we drive up the coast and get to this amazing house that's all glass and chrome and is perched on a cliff overlooking the ocean and there's this pool that looks like it flows off of the cliff—an infinity pool. It looks like it just goes on and on forever.

Ian's friend Blake answered the door barefoot in designer jeans and a bright green Lacoste polo that was tight around his biceps. He was handsome and had brown hair that was short on the sides and messy on top. Ian introduced him to Ross and then me.

When I walked in, Blake smiled at me almost like he was shy. Then he took my hand and said that Ian was the best friend in the world for bringing the prettiest girl to his party.

I was like WHAT? I looked over at Ross, who winked at me and laughed. Blake slid my hand around his arm like he was walking me down the aisle at a wedding and gave us the full tour. It was really crowded already. People were everywhere, and it seemed as if Blake knew every single one of them.

Upstairs in the master suite, Blake slid open the big glass wall and led me out onto the balcony, and Ian and Ross followed us. The view was so amazing that it took my breath away. I asked Blake what it was like to wake up in that bed and see this view every morning, and he turned and looked right at me and said, Why don't you stay tonight and find out?

I blushed really hard. I jerked my arm away from him and put my hands up to my cheeks. I didn't want to, but I couldn't help it! I felt so strange inside. Ian laughed and Ross whistled, and I just didn't understand what was happening. I mean, Blake is very, very handsome, and he's not that much older than I am. He just turned 20, so he's like 3½ years older than me, but I really like Ross, and I couldn't understand why he was whistling and hooting, and it sort of made me mad at him because I realized that he wasn't acting like he liked me back very much.

When we got back downstairs, new people had arrived with bottles of white wine and vodka. Blake led the way into the kitchen, which was as nice as the master bedroom. It was like something out of a magazine. I looked around at all of the people who were there, and I pulled Ross aside while Ian was making us drinks and whispered, WOW we're like the youngest people here.

He smiled at me and said, I know! Isn't it better than those dumb high school parties?

I stepped out the big glass doors off the kitchen toward the pool to get a closer look. There were already a lot of people outside, and I walked down to the end where the pool seemed to flow over the edge of the cliff and looked past the clear glass partition at the edge of the pool area. The water flowed over a false edge into a trough below where it was sucked back into the pool filtration system. It created a pretty little waterfall.

When I turned around, there were two girls standing behind me, admiring the view. I say girls, but one was older than the other. She must've been in her 30s but she was dressed much younger. Her hair was red, but I don't think it was her natural color. She was standing next to a tall blond girl who looked like she was about my age, only she had really long legs and wore a short black dress. She was holding a beer, and she looked like a high schooler on a TV show—you know, one of those shows where high school girls are really pretty and have million-dollar wardrobes and no zits, and they're constantly getting their moms out of trouble instead of getting into trouble themselves? Anyway, she looked like that, and when I turned around, I realized that she was closer to my age than anyone else at the party besides Ross.

Both girls smiled and said hi. The blond girl told me her name was Lauren. I introduced myself and then turned back to follow her gaze back out across the water. We both stared for a minute in silence, and then she said how amazing this place was. I smiled and agreed. The redhead said her name was Diane and asked who I was there with. I told her I was there with Ross. She asked if that was the guy who came with Ian, and I said yes. Lauren asked me how long I'd known Ross, and I told her we'd been going out for a couple of weeks. This made Diane start laughing really hard, and Lauren sort of looked at me like she felt sorry for me and elbowed Diane in the ribs.

I asked what was so funny. Lauren looked at me and said: Ross is gay.

I stood there at the end of the pool, and the first thought I had when she said it was that I was glad there was a glass partition behind me to keep me from falling over the edge of the cliff. I. COULDN'T. BELIEVE IT.

Diane was still laughing and told Lauren to come inside with her because there were a bunch of people Diane needed to introduce her to. She tried to grab Lauren's arm, but Lauren didn't even look at her. Just rolled her eyes and shook Diane off her arm. She told Diane to go ahead, that she'd come in a minute. Diane told her to hurry and then walked back toward the house.

I turned back around toward the ocean and closed my eyes really tight. I thought maybe Lauren would just take the hint and follow Diane back into the house. I didn't want her to see me cry. I didn't want to cry, but I couldn't help it. I knew that my mascara was going to run and I'd look like a raccoon.

I felt Lauren walk up next to me, so I opened my eyes. She was staring out at the ocean and the lights on the coastline in the distance. She was quiet for a minute, then I felt her pat me on the back and say, All the cute ones are gay. I tried to smile, but I was so embarrassed.

When I was quiet, she just kept talking—like it was easy. I could tell she was one of those girls who could talk to anybody. I usually hate them because sometimes it's really hard for me to speak up, but I was glad that she was there. Otherwise it would have just been me crying over the edge of the cliff at a party where I should have been having fun. I HATE that about myself. Most of the time I feel like everyone else is cooler and smarter and prettier than I am. It was nice that she was talking to me because it gave me a second to chill out and just listen.

Lauren told me that when she'd first met Ross at that party on the beach with Ian, she thought he was really cute too. And she told me not to feel bad because she'd thought he was straight 'cause of the truck and the surfboards and everything. She told me that she was new to town, too. She'd just moved here from New York to live with her dad. His name is Gerald (with a hard G, not a J sound) and he's a music producer. Blake's dad is a movie producer, so basically he is a rich kid who grew up in the Palisades. He dropped out of NYU and started a band. Lauren used to sneak out of the house in New York to go to Blake's shows, and she told her dad about his band. Her dad came with her to a show one night and signed the band, so Blake moved back out to Los Angeles.

I asked Lauren why she moved to Los Angeles. She was quiet for a minute, then looked at me and told me that she came to live with her dad because her mom's boyfriend in New York was a total creep who kept hitting on her. She took a sip of her beer, then offered it to me. I smiled at her and told her that I don't like beer.

She laughed really loudly and said, ME NEITHER, then reached over and poured the rest of her beer into the pool. I started laughing too, and it felt good to laugh with somebody. Lauren said C'mon and grabbed my hand and pulled me back toward the house. I asked her where we were going, and she said to find some good stuff.

I couldn't believe how cool Lauren was and that she was being so nice to me.

Lauren gave Diane the slip again, weaving past her near the door to the house. She said Diane worked at the label for her dad. Diane was trying to introduce Lauren to people, supposedly because Lauren was new in town, but really so that Diane could pretend to be important and cool by running around with her boss's daughter.

Lauren led us to the bar in the kitchen where Blake was mixing drinks. Ian and Ross were there, passing a joint back and forth. Ross came over and gave me a hug and kiss on the cheek. He said he was so glad Lauren and I had met each other. Lauren rolled her eyes and jabbed him in the ribs.

What was that for? Ross wanted to know.

Lauren said it was for being a heartbreaker and that we weren't here for hot gay guys, we were here for cosmos.

Blake laughed hard when she said that, shouted COMIN' RIGHT UP, then started pouring vodka and cranberry and some other stuff into a martini shaker. I had never had a cosmo, just seen them on TV. The women drinking them were always wearing high heels like Lauren's, and they didn't ever seem to feel ugly or at a loss for words, like me. I looked around at Ian and Blake and Ross and Lauren, and all of a sudden I didn't feel like a loser anymore.

Blake passed me a martini glass with cold pink liquid about to slosh over the rim. I took a small sip off the top as he held it. It was SO GOOD! It was sweet, but not syrupy like wine coolers. It was so cold and a little tart, but then as I swallowed it, I felt the warmth of the vodka all the way down. Blake grinned at me over the rim of the glass, like we were sharing a secret. He told me I had perfect lips, and when he said it, I blushed. AGAIN. He was so cute and had this little dimple when he smiled halfway. He actually reminded me a little bit of stupid Nathan—only Blake is MUCH COOLER.

By the time I finished that drink in the kitchen with Lauren, I was feeling SO BUZZED. It was so much fun, and Blake had cranked up the music in the living room. Ross grabbed Lauren's hand and reached for mine, and I pulled my hand back like Ross was a hot stove. I felt this weird stab in my chest and just looked at him. No matter how much I didn't want to feel it, I was hurt; hurt that he hadn't mentioned he was gay; embarrassed that I hadn't figured it out; afraid that he thought I was stupid for having a crush on him.

He must've seen it in my eyes, 'cause he tossed his bangs in that little way he always does, and said, I have to dance with you right now.

I crossed my arms, and said, Why?

He said because it's a rule that the gay dude has to dance with the two hottest girls at the party, and Lauren's already coming, so that just leaves you.

I peered up at him through my lashes and said, I flat-ironed my hair at 6 a.m. for you that first day we went to the beach.

Lauren threw her head back and laughed so hard she snorted. That made me start giggling, and suddenly I was leaning against Ross to keep from falling down. We all laughed so hard we almost cried, and just like that, with a group hug and a good laugh, all of the embarrassment melted away, and I realized that there was something better than making out with Ross would ever be: dancing with him at this party.

Blake followed us into the living room that ran the length of the house. It had gotten dark outside finally, and the pool was lit up, flowing over the edge of the cliff. The moon was high in the sky, and I felt so good! The cosmo made my head feel all warm and I was laughing with Lauren as we sandwiched Ross between us and danced with our hands up in the air.

Blake danced up behind me and I felt his hands on my waist. My heart started beating really fast, and at first I pulled away a little, but then he gently pulled me back into him and whispered in my ear. He said, I don't bite, and I laughed, and then he said, At least not hard anyway, and that made me smile.

I leaned my head back against his chest and he wrapped his arms around my waist and I felt him pressed up against me. I could barely breathe!

The doorbell rang, and someone answered, and a another big group of Blake's friends found us in the living room. As Blake kissed and fist-bumped and high-fived his way around the room, Lauren came dancing over and whisper-yelled over the music, OMG! BLAKE LIKES YOU SO MUCH. Then she said, C'mon let's go get more cosmos.

So we did.

Lauren's cosmos tasted as good as Blake's did! I asked her how she learned, and she just flipped a long strand of blond hair over her shoulder and raised her eyebrow. She said that some girls are scouts and learn how to sew buttons and tie knots. She'd been mixing drinks for her mom since she was 12.

We danced our way back to the living room with our glasses and danced with these two really tall guys who were twins, for what seemed like hours. As we danced, I kept looking over at Lauren and thinking how comfortable she was with all of this, and then I realized: SURPRISE! YOU'RE comfortable with all of this, and it felt so AMAZING. I knew that this wasn't just me being there with Lauren. It was the cosmos. They totally helped! I'd always heard all of this stuff about how dangerous it was to drink and how many teenagers get killed in drunk driving accidents, but no one ever told me how it actually FEELS to be buzzed on cosmos and dancing with two hot guys and your new friend at a party overlooking the ocean!

Somehow my glass kept getting refilled and it felt like we were dancing for hours. I was feeling really buzzed when one of the twins asked Lauren if we wanted to come outside with them for a cigarette. Lauren just laughed and said that tobacco was totally gross. Then she blew the twins a kiss and dragged me upstairs, giggling.

When we got to the master bedroom, Blake was leaning over a mirror on the bedside table. I didn't really see what he was doing, but when he saw us, he popped up and rubbed his nose, sniffing, and said LADIES! really loud, like us coming in was the best thing that had ever happened. Lauren sort of froze and was looking down at the bedside table. I followed her gaze and there was a mirror sitting there with a little pile of white powder on it. I was FREAKING OUT! I didn't even know anybody who KNEW anybody who did cocaine, and now there was a pile of it sitting right in front of us.

I felt an arm come around my waist and somebody kissed my neck, and I turned around to see Ross. When I saw him, he pinched my stomach, and it tickled, so I giggled and twisted around. Right then Blake pointed at the mirror and asked Lauren if she wanted to do a line. I guess he meant sniff a line of cocaine because I'd never actually heard anyone offer someone cocaine, much less SEEN IT RIGHT THERE IN FRONT OF ME!!!

I sort of held my breath. Ross was watching Lauren too. She flipped her hair over her shoulder and said, WE aren't doing any REAL drugs. But I might show a little leg for a joint! Ross whooped and shouted TAKE IT OFF, BABY! and pulled a little tinfoil pouch out of his pocket, waving it around. Blake cracked up, and before I knew it, he had set up this really big glass tube with about 3 inches of water in the bottom. Ross called it a bong and gave me a step-by-step on what he was doing as he loaded some brown powdery stuff into the tiny bowl on the side.

I was feeling all spinny from the cosmos, and when I saw the brown powder in the tinfoil I said, Oh no! Ross, your weed went bad. It's all brown! and everybody cracked up. Blake came over and told me I was his new favorite girl and that this was called hash—which Ross said is like just the part of marijuana that makes you get high, or something like that. I can't really remember. All I knew was that Lauren said if I liked pot, I'd REEEEEEEALLY like hash.

SHE.

WAS.

RIGHT!

OMG.

I took one hit off of the bong, and the smoke didn't even make me cough. When I smoked joints with Ross, it took a couple minutes to feel anything. Maybe it was 'cause I'd already drank three cosmos, or maybe it was just 'cause this was hash, but it hit me—WHAM! The minute I blew the smoke out I felt SO HIGH.

Only, this high was DIFFERENT. I didn't feel paranoid, like I sometimes do when I smoke pot. I just felt floaty, and good. I'm not really sure how we got downstairs, because the next thing I remember is Lauren kicking off her high heels and standing up on the diving board with me. Blake had turned the music on the outside speakers up really loud, and Blake and Lauren and I started dancing on the diving board.

Lauren saw the twins and jumped down to run over and say hi, and then it was just me and Blake dancing on the diving board over the pool. I could see Ian and Ross were down by the edge where the pool seemed to drop over the cliff. Ross had his arms around Ian's neck, and there was this smile on his face that made me feel so good inside.

I spun around a little too fast, though, and I guess I was drunker than I thought, or maybe it was the hash, but the next thing I knew I had fallen in the water. And the most AMAZING thing happened: I started laughing. I mean, usually I'd have just fallen apart from embarrassment and wanted to just drown. CAN YOU BELIEVE IT? Falling off the diving board right in front of a WHOLE PARTY full of people staring at me like that?

The water felt cool against my skin, not too cold, and I saw all of these bubbles burst up in front of my face and realized that I was laughing. I was laughing at myself, and how silly it was that I was dancing on a diving board with a 20-year-old boy anyway, and then OF COURSE that I was the klutz who would fall into the water, and it felt AMAZING!

Of course, it only took me about 10 seconds to think all of this, but the hash was still playing with my sense of time, I think, because it felt like quite a while. Only, I wasn't panicked from being in the water, just laughing at myself, and then through the bubbles from my laughter, I saw another body splash into the pool and then swim toward me. It was BLAKE! He had jumped in with all of his clothes on too, and I felt his arms around me as we swam up to the surface.

When our heads popped out of the water, I heard the music again and I heard Blake laughing. I turned toward him as Blake found his footing near the shallower end of the middle of the pool. He pulled me closer and said, Gotta be careful dancing on the diving board. He said it with a big sweet smile. Then he leaned in and kissed me. I closed my eyes and just felt weightless in the water, with Blake's arms wrapped around my waist and my legs tangled up in his.

Ross and Lauren were suddenly at the edge of the pool, and Ross shouted, OH JEEZ! Come up for air you two! And then I heard Lauren giggle, and I looked up just as she pushed Ross into the pool, then jumped in herself. All of a sudden the whole place turned into a POOL PARTY and about 20 people were in the pool with their clothes on, laughing and shrieking, and in the middle of it all Blake and I were floating around kissing. I can't remember when I've EVER had more fun in my entire LIFE.

After a while Blake helped me out of the pool and we went upstairs to get towels. When we were in his bathroom, he took off his shirt and jeans right there in front of me, like it was no big deal. He draped a white robe over my shoulders. Then we kissed for a long time. OMG! I HAD NEVER KISSED A GUY IN JUST HIS UNDERWEAR. He was just wearing a pair of black briefs, which I thought was sort of sexy because most high school guys wear boxers. Not that I've seen a lot of them except when their jeans are riding low. But Blake's underwear looked sort of expensive and made him seem like a grown-up. I was leaning up against the sink, and Blake was breathing really heavily. I could feel that he was hard through his underwear and it was pressed right up against me. I made out with Sean last year when we went to homecoming, and it was the same thing, but Sean was wearing jeans at the time, and he was kissing me like he was going to swallow half of my face. Blake is a MUCH better kisser, and he was kissing my neck and giving me goose bumps all up and down my arms (even WITH the robe on) when I heard Ian calling my name and coming up the stairs.

That's when I remembered I had a curfew.

Blake wasn't too happy that I had to be home so early. He kept pulling me closer to him and whispering "don't go" into my ear, but I finally giggled and pushed him away. Back downstairs, Ross, Lauren, and Blake traded cell numbers for everybody. Lauren kept laughing and hugging me and saying OMG! I'm so happy we met! We're going to have so much fun!

As I headed downstairs in my soggy clothes, my head was starting to feel a little heavy, like I couldn't hold it up by myself. Blake leaned in for one last kiss and whispered, When will I see you again? in my ear. I tried to say "soon," but the room was kind of spinning and it was like my tongue was made of a big cotton ball, only it was heavy and I couldn't make it move the way I wanted it to. Ross was laughing and said, C'mon, princess, let's get you to the car.

Somehow I got to the backseat of Ian's SUV, because the next thing I remember is Ross yelling, WHOA WHOA

61

WHOA, and Ian must've pulled over, because I felt the car swerve and then stop really fast. Ross opened the door, and I leaned over and barfed really hard onto the curb. My head was pounding, and Ross was there, helping me sit back up in the car.

I remember pulling up to our house, and I tried to get out, but Ross wouldn't let me. He was texting someone on his phone, and the last thing I really remember is Cam coming to the door of the SUV and telling me that I had to be quiet. I don't know what I was saying, really.

When I woke up this morning, I was in bed, and my head hurt so bad, I thought I might throw up again. I went into the bathroom and took some Advil and lay back down again. I must've drifted off, because I just woke up again to my phone buzzing. I have 3 text messages: Ross, Lauren, and Blake. THAT put a big smile on my face just now. I'm SO EXCITED to hang out with all of them again. I want Cam to meet them too. He'd love Blake, I think.

Only next time, no hash when I've had 3 cosmos. UGH. I don't EVER want my head to hurt like this again.

Later . . .

ARGH. Sometimes I just hate Cam so much.

He is soooooooo pissed about last night. He said that he was almost asleep when he got a text from Ross that I was wasted and that he had to come get me out. He asked me if I even remembered walking into the house. I said yes, but I don't, and he knew it. He asked me if I remembered talking to Mom and Dad and I said of course I did, and he just shook his head and glared at me and said Mom and Dad were in BED. Then he called me an idiot under his breath.

I don't see what the big deal is. I mean, they don't know I came home drunk, and they're not going to find out. I told Cam he should just calm down. He said, CALM DOWN? You came home last night in a BLACKOUT.

I don't really think it was a blackout. I mean, I still remember most everything. I think a blackout is like when you wake up somewhere and you don't know how you got there, right? Either way, I got sort of scared when I saw how upset Cam was, plus my head still hurt and my stomach felt really gross. I started to cry a little bit, and Cam chilled out. He brought me some orange juice and told me that I had to be smarter about partying, but he was still really serious about everything.

I just don't understand why he has to be like that. I mean, nothing happened. Next time I'll just drink more slowly, and I won't smoke hash on top of it. It's really no big deal.

Lauren just texted me. She said she had fun last night and I should call her when I'm up.

She didn't seem too drunk at all last night. I wonder if she has some tips for not getting quite so wasted? OMG. LOL. Maybe I just won't drink ever again. Jeez. I'm gonna call Lauren. That'll make me feel better.

OH! AND! I'm going to pack for VACATION next week! That'll make me feel better for SURE!

July 28

Blake keeps texting me!

Okay, he's not really texting, he's sexting—all about how he wants to kiss me again. He said he wants to be in the pool with me again, only this time just us, and we'll take our clothes off first.

I sorta blushed when I read that one.

Lauren says he's a horn-dog and Ross says that he's a cokehead.

But I kinda can't stop thinking about him. I keep replaying that scene in his bathroom in my mind, and I get that same feeling, like I can't quite catch my breath, and my pulse races. Then he'll send me a text about wanting to feel my body against his or something, and I get all embarrassed by it, and nervous— like I'm ashamed of it. Yesterday the text he sent me just grossed me out, and I didn't even text him back.

It's confusing. I want him to like me and I want him to be

turned on by me, but I feel like the cosmos and the pot got me to jump way past this place where it was flirty and fun, and we wound up almost naked in his bathroom. Now it all seems to mean more somehow, or maybe I just want it to mean more?

Maybe it only means more to me, and I feel like every text he sends me is all about my body. That's why I feel weird about it. I'm not sure if likes anything besides my body.

Does that make me one of those crazy girls who is always asking for MORE? I mean, I only hung out with him ONE TIME, and now I am a complete LUNATIC thinking about him ALL THE TIME—his body in those little black briefs, the way he felt pressed up against me.

Maybe I just need to hang out with him again and see what happens. I want to, but he hasn't really texted me to ask me out on a date or anything. Maybe I can see if Lauren can set something up so we can all go hang out together.

July 29

Today was my last day of geometry summer school!

Cam dropped me off this morning, and Lauren and Ross were waiting for me when I got done taking the test. I'm pretty sure I aced it. And if I didn't, WHO CARES??? At least the tutoring with stupid Nathan paid off. Glad I got something out of that guy. HA HA HA!

Ross and Lauren and I drove down the beach and passed a pipe around. I asked Ross where he gets his weed because I feel like I smoke a lot of it lately. (Am I a total stoner now?) He said he gets it from Ian. Lauren said she's going to try to get a medical marijuana card so that we can go get it legally. I'd never thought about that before.

After we were good and stoned, we decided to drive up the highway along the water. Ross rolled down the windows and Lauren turned up the music, and I let my arm drift out the window. For a second I wondered if it was a good idea for Ross to be driving around stoned, but I couldn't worry about it for even 5 seconds. It was one of those beautiful days when the sky is so blue that you can't believe it's real, like you're watching a movie of the sky. The long grass on the hills along the road was yellowed from being baked in the sun all summer. I just decided it was too beautiful out to worry about Ross, or anything else, for that matter. I told myself that driving stoned is different from driving drunk. I've heard about drunk driving accidents, but I've never heard of a stoned driving accident. Besides, the breeze off the ocean was cool and everything smelled fresh. The salt air whipping through the truck, through my hair, through my fingers seemed to carry every worry away.

Ross pulled the truck off the road into a little parking lot by one of the state beaches and led the way down a flight of railroad tie stairs onto a stretch of sandy beach at the base of a steep cliff. At one end of the beach were huge rocks and boulders that led to a small cave where we could walk through to a secluded stretch of private beach (if we ducked). When the tide was out, you could make it through. Ross said we could hang for an hour before the water got too high to walk through.

We were the only ones on the beach. Lauren pulled off her top. Ross stripped down to his boxers and they both teased me until I took off my shirt too. At first I was like HELL NO, but then Lauren rolled her eyes, and said, Oh, c'mon, it's not like he's checking you out or anything. She had a point, I decided.

Lauren and I sat there next to each other in our bras, staring out at the water while Ross jumped into the waves and body surfed for a little while. (OMG. Lauren's body is CRAZY. She's so skinny!) After a while Ross came out of the water, all dripping, and golden brown, and gorgeous. He sat down, and the three of us started talking about school. Turns out Ross and Lauren are BOTH coming to my high school! I HADN'T EVEN THOUGHT ABOUT THAT! This school year is going to be SO GREAT!

They both had lots of questions about teachers and what the kids were like and who my friends were. I was sorta embarrassed because I told them that I didn't have many close friends and that I was really glad they were both going to be there. Lauren asked why I didn't have a lot of friends. She seems like one of those people who makes friends really easily without even trying that hard.

I told them I didn't know why I had a harder time making friends. I'm quieter than Cam is, I guess. I said that people seem so unpredictable to me, and that scares me. Ross laughed and said that he finds people TOTALLY predictable. I smiled and said that it really helped to smoke some pot. And also that Lauren's cosmos helped me be less quiet.

This made Lauren giggle until there were tears running down her face, and Ross laughed too. He said the funniest thing he'd seen all summer was the moment I fell off the diving board at Blake's house, and I started laughing too. We all lay there laughing for a long time. We'd finally get quiet, and then one of us would think about it again and start giggling all over, until finally my stomach hurt.

On the way home, Lauren and Ross took turns quizzing me about Blake, and Lauren almost made Ross run off the road while she tickled me until I gave her my phone so she could read all of the texts that Blake had sent me. Ross wanted to know if I was going to see Blake again, and I said I didn't know how to work that out. My parents would NEVER go for me dating a 20-year-old. I think that's part of the reason that it feels so EXCITING when he texts me: It feels dangerous. Lauren is going to see if she can set up another party with Blake when I get back from vacation.

When Ross dropped me off, Lauren said she was really going to miss me while I was away. Ross said he would too. I made them promise not to have too much fun without me.

July 31

It's so early in the morning I can barely keep my eyes open. Somehow I made it to the gate at LAX with Mom and Dad and Cam. Cam just asked me if I wanted to come with him to get coffee. I don't like coffee that much, but maybe I can get a vanilla latte. Ugh. How come vacation feels like a chore right now?

Later . . .

I never realized how much people drink on airplanes. The people sitting across the aisle from me and Cam are having Bloody Marys. They've both had 2, and the guy just ordered another one. It's, like, midmorning and this flight isn't that long. They're going to be wasted by the time we land.

I wonder what it would be like to drink on a plane?

I've really only drank once. I don't count that wine cooler at the party, but now I notice it more when other people are doing it. Last night at dinner Mom and Dad each had a glass of wine.

I sat there the whole time wondering what wine tastes like. I thought about sneaking a sip after dinner, but then Lauren called, and I forgot about it.

Later . . .

We just had lunch at a restaurant in the airport because our rental car was delayed.

EVERYONE was drinking. Except me and Cam.

Dad had a beer. Mom had a glass of chardonnay. Well, Dad convinced her to. He laughed and said, C'MON! We're on vacation, Margaret! She acted all giggly like she was going to get caught by the wine police or something.

Cam said that it was cocktail hour SOMEWHERE in the world. Mom shot him a look and said, Well, it's not cocktail hour for EITHER of you for at least another few years.

She. Would. Have. A. FIT. If. She. Found. Out.

Maybe I should start hiding this journal. I don't think Mom would ever go snooping. Still . . . Oh! Our flight's boarding.

Blake just texted me AGAIN:

THINK OF ME WHEN U RUB IN UR SUNSCREEN.

God. He's such a dirty boy!!!

(I kinda LIKE IT!!!)

August 2

Mexico is AMAZING.

We drove for about 30 minutes up the coast to this little beach town. Dad rented a house on the water here. The house isn't as nice as ours at home, but it's RIGHT on the beach! When we got here, there were two women in the kitchen who work at the house and make food and clean everything. It's like a hotel only the food is included and it's a lot cheaper to just rent the house for a week.

I am sitting writing this in a little hut that is right on the beach in front of the house. It's nicer than a hut, really. It's just a thatched roof over beautiful tile—sort of like a gazebo, only no walls or lattice. There's a little bar with a sink and some stools next to a grill, and big cushions on built-in benches all around the perimeter that face the water. I watched Cam head down the beach with a surfboard a few minutes ago.

It's so strange being in a place where my phone doesn't work at all. I didn't realize how much I'd been texting Ross and Lauren in the past few days. Or Blake. It's funny; when I think of him my heart races, but I'm not sure I even like him. I feel like he's the ocean and I've fallen in and the waves are too big; like I'm in over my head. I'm not even sure which way is up anymore.

All I can see in front of me is water. The beach seems to go on for miles, and miles. The sound of the waves hitting the shore is loud and the rhythm makes me take deep breaths. Everything just feels slower here—more relaxed.

Except for the waves, it's so quiet.

August 3

Today was so FUN! Dad booked this thing called a canopy tour for us and we went zip-lining through the trees. It was scary at first, but it made my heart race in a really fun way. That feeling of free falling really fast for just a few seconds always takes my breath away. It's SO SCARY, but SO FUN. When I was on, I looked down like 5 stories and thought, AM I REALLY ABOUT TO DO THIS??? I couldn't believe it, but I just jumped!

WWWWHHHHHHHHEEEEEEEEEEEEEEEEEE!

It was SO. MUCH. FUN!!! As soon as I did it, I couldn't wait to do it again.

Can't wait for dinner! I'm STARVING. The food here is SO GOOD. Tonight the cooks said they were making something called ceviche that is fish and lemon juice and other stuff. I can't wait to try it!

August 4

I fell asleep on the beach this afternoon, and I would've gotten SO sunburned except Mom came down to join me and woke me up just as I was starting to get a little pink. She rubbed some sunscreen into my shoulders, and then I did her back. It was actually fun to lie on the beach with her. She told me she thought Ross was really sweet. I told her about meeting Lauren at the party. At first I was worried that she was going to start grilling me, but she didn't! She said she was really glad that I'd made a friend, and she was excited to meet her.

I also told her that Ross was gay. She just smiled and asked me how I felt about that. All of a sudden I felt really close to her, like my opinion really mattered to her. I told her that I was confused at first because he hadn't told me right away and he was such a guy's guy. He liked surfing and sports and drove a truck and everything. Anyway, we talked for a long time. She told me about this guy she'd dated in high school who wound up coming out when he went to college, and the story was so funny. Maybe not the story, but the way she told it. It was like we were girlfriends sharing secrets.

Dad was reading up in the little hut-gazebo thing and came down after a while of hearing us laughing. He brought Mom a margarita and me a Diet Coke. We all sat there on the beach and watched Cam riding waves. It felt so good to be there with them, to feel like I was part of something special.

We had dinner outside tonight. Dad grilled burgers in the little outdoor kitchen. We all lounged around and ate until we were stuffed as the sun set over the ocean. Mom and Dad just went for a walk down the beach together after it got dark, and Cam is up at the house watching a movie.

I'm just sitting here listening to the ocean, thinking about how lucky I am that my mom and dad are still together, and how fun this trip is. And look! No drinking or drugs required. Mom left almost a full margarita after dinner, and I thought about trying a sip of it when she and Dad left on their walk, but you know what?

I'm good.

Just like this.

Just where I am.

August 6

Back on a plane.

Back to cell phone signals!

Next stop: home.

Later . . .

OMG.

Like a MILLION texts popped up on my phone the minute we landed.

Okay, not a million, but a lot.

A lot were from Ross and Lauren. Most of them were from

Blake. Blake sent me texts every single day. Lots of them. And every single night, he sent even more. Blake sent me a lot of texts in the middle of the night. The later the texts, the sexier they were. I was sitting next to my mom as the plane taxied to the gate, and I had to put my phone away because I didn't want her to see any of the really sexy ones. He texted me pictures of himself. Shirtless. And more. It's weird. I'm not really sure why guys think girls want to see that. I mean, I guess it's one thing to feel it pressed up against me in his bathroom, but . . .

I dunno.

Leave something to my imagination, will you?

August 8

Mom met Lauren yesterday, and she really liked her, which is very good news for me. That means I don't have to worry about Mom hassling me about hanging out with her. Lauren lives with her dad in this gorgeous condo near the water. I didn't mention to Mom that Lauren's dad is out of town a lot. He's constantly flying back to New York. I've just sort of let that go because I know Mom's rule that if I'm spending the night at a friend's house a parent needs to be there. It's such a lame, old-fashioned rule.

After we hung out at our house for a while, Lauren asked if I wanted to spend the night. Mom said as long as it was okay with Lauren's dad, it was fine with her. Lauren assured her that it was fine with her dad. Lauren's dad is in New York this weekend, so he won't even know, but obviously we didn't tell Mom that. The best part is that Lauren's dad has plenty of Absolut and Lauren made us cosmos. Ross came over and we all had a couple of drinks and smoked pot out of Ross's pipe. Ian came over too, and brought more weed because Ross was low.

It was SO FUN to be back with the gang! I couldn't stop thinking about Blake and texted him to tell him that we were all hanging out. He texted me back FAST and said he wanted to come but he was in San Francisco playing a show with his band. Lauren smirked and asked me who I was texting, really loudly in front of everyone because she already knew, and my face got totally red and they all whistled and teased me about dating an older man.

I said, We are NOT dating.

Lauren laughed, and said, Not YET anyway. Just wait until NEXT SATURDAY!

Ian smiled, and I could tell he knew what Lauren was talking about. I asked what next Saturday was, and Lauren said, We're going HIKING with your BOYFRIEND . . .

I was like, Hiking? Why are we going hiking? We'll be all sweaty and gross! I want him to think I'm pretty, not a big sweat ball.

Lauren poured more cosmo into my glass and said that we

weren't just hiking, that there would be a special surprise. Blake's uncle has a ranch up the coast and there are all of these trails through the foothills and even some horses that run free on the back acres. We are going to drive up and spend the day. I am excited but a little worried about spending a whole day with Blake. At least it won't be a hard sell for my mom. What could be more wholesome than a daytime hiking trip?

August 9

Cam can't go hiking with us because he has to clean pools all day. He's bummed. And I am too, a little. Blake keeps texting me about how much fun this hike is going to be. It's weird, but I never thought of Blake as much of an outdoors guy. Maybe this has to do with the big SURPRISE that Lauren keeps talking about. It's making me nervous. I wish she'd just tell me already, but she says that it would no longer then (by definition) be a surprise.

August 12

Lauren is spending the night so that we can get up first thing in the morning and get on the road to Blake's place up the coast, then get on the road to his uncle's ranch. It's about an hour's drive past his place, according to Lauren. I told her that we were NOT going to talk about Blake to my Mom and she gets it.

Mom is THRILLED that we are going hiking with Ian and Ross. Lauren told her that the ranch we're going to is owned by a friend of her dad's, which is sort of half true. I mean, technically, her dad DOES know who Blake's dad is, and knows that the ranch is in Blake's family. Anyway, Mom has packed us a cooler of sandwiches and cans of Diet Coke, and bottles of water, and made us promise to take lots of pictures, and call when we're headed back.

Cam is all mopey that he can't come. I told him he should just call in sick tomorrow, but Cam is very conscientious and says he needs the money.

August 13

Wow.

W-O-W.

I'm not even sure where to start.

When Lauren and I got to Blake's house, Ian and Ross were already there. I guess they'd spent the night there. I'd been chattering nonstop to Lauren all the way there about how crazy nervous I was about seeing Blake again, and what if this was all in my head, and Blake didn't really like me at all. She just rolled her eyes and said that I was very good at inventing reasons to be worried.

The minute he opened the door, Blake wrapped both arms

around me and kissed me on the lips really gently. He smiled and said, Finally. Then he sort of danced me into the kitchen so he could grab some water bottles. Lauren giggled and yelled TOLD YOU as she ran upstairs to get Ross and Ian. In the kitchen, Blake leaned me up against the island and kissed me so firmly that my knees went a little bit weak, and I was glad that I was leaning against something solid. He pressed his whole body into mine, and I could smell his skin, and the body wash he must've used, and the product in his hair that smelled like eucalyptus.

All of the worries I'd had about him melted inside of me. It raced out of me from every direction, through a buzz under my skin that came shooting out of my fingers and toes and the hair at the top of my head. What was left after all of the doubts were gone was the sound of my heart pounding in my ears and the heat of Blake's breath on my skin.

In that moment I just didn't care whether he wanted to date me or not; I knew that he liked me totally and completely, and I wanted to just stay right there with him all day long, kissing in the kitchen.

When we heard Lauren and the boys coming down the stairs, he grabbed my hand and dragged me out to the driveway with him. We all piled into Ian's SUV, then headed north up the coast to the ranch. When I took the cooler out of Lauren's car,

Ian asked me what it was, and I told him it was food and drinks for the trip. Ian laughed, and Blake said, We probably won't need any food today, but the drinks will come in handy.

I didn't understand what they meant right away, but once we got to the ranch and Blake jumped out to open the gate at the end of the gravel road we'd taken off of the highway, Ian turned around and said, Okay everybody! Time for the hiking surprise!

He pulled a Ziploc bag out of his pocket and handed it to Ross. We parked the SUV under a tree at the edge of a giant meadow that had a little gravelly stream running through it. The stream looked like it wound up into the hills, which were covered in tall, sun-bleached grass, yellow and waving in the breeze. The sky was bright blue and the clouds were big white billows, wafting slowly behind the mountains in the distance.

Lauren was passing around sunscreen for our faces and ears, and she helped me spread it onto the part in my hair so that I wouldn't get burned there, either. I started wondering how long we were going to be out in the sun, and when I asked Blake, he took my hand and said, Well, it all depends on how long the surprise lasts.

Ross and Ian had everybody huddle up and hold out our hands. Ross dropped one tiny square of white paper into each of our palms, and Ian told us not to drop it because this is all that there was, and he'd been through HELL trying to get it.

I asked what it was, and Blake said, It's LSD.

My eyes went wide as I saw Ross hand the plastic bag back to Ian, and then gently place the little square of paper on his tongue. I almost shouted, This is ACID? We're going to take ACID?

Ross giggled and said, We're taking a little trip today.

Blake rubbed his hand on my back and said, It's okay. I'll be right here.

Lauren laughed and said, C'mon! You're going to LOVE it.

I wasn't sure what to expect, but when I put the little square on my tongue, it tasted like . . . nothing. I looked at Ross for a minute, and then at Blake. I asked if something was supposed to happen.

Ian laughed, and said, Not yet. It'll kick in after about 15 or 20 minutes. Let's go hike!

Blake led the way down the trail along the little stream, which looked like it must have more water in it during the spring. Right now it was just a little trickle that ran over a few of the rocks at the center. We hiked along the stream for a while. Ross was running and jumping onto Ian's back and making him give him a piggyback ride for a few feet every so often. Lauren and Blake and I were walking together, and Blake had his arm draped over my neck.

After a little while the stream dipped in between two hills

and the trail led up the side of one of them. As we climbed up, I was telling Blake and Lauren all about our vacation to Mexico, and it must've taken a little while because I was just talking and talking, then we reached the top of the hill and I realized that I was breathing sort of fast, and when I lifted my eyes up from the path, I stopped midsentence and sucked in a huge deep breath of air. We were standing at the top of the hill and I could see the blue sky and the rolling hills of the valley below. The place where the blue sky met the yellow grass seemed miles away in the distance, dotted with bright, brilliant green trees, and when I stared out at the white clouds, they seemed to breathe in and then collapse a little, then breathe in again.

Then the green trees at the horizon begin to wriggle in this strange way, almost like they were dancing with one another. They would swirl together and reach up toward the white clouds, and then the clouds would answer back, swirling down toward the green trees, and all at once I was LAUGHING. I gasped and gulped in the air and I said, You guys, LOOK! The trees and the clouds are DANCING!

Lauren and Blake walked up on either side of me and I grabbed both of their hands and said, SEE?

We just stood there for what must've been an hour, or maybe it was 5 minutes? I don't know! That's the amazing thing about acid; you just can't tell how much time has passed. It's like someone has shuffled all the cards in your head, and you recognize people and places, but you can't quite fit together how you got here, or where you are, only that you feel AMAZING, and you're seeing these INCREDIBLE THINGS.

While we stood and watched the trees and the clouds, Ross and Ian suddenly let out a whoop and went racing down the hill through the yellow grass into the valley below, and as we followed them, I saw the yellow grass around me. I stuck out my hands as we ran and let my fingers brush through the tall thin stalks, only it felt like liquid running over my hands.

At the bottom of the hill we found Ian and Ross sitting next to each other on their knees in the middle of the tall grass. They had mashed down a little place in a circle, and they were sitting there, holding hands. Ian said, Look! We built a NEST.

Lauren and Blake and I saw this and laughed and laughed until the tears ran down our cheeks. I thought it was amazing and wonderful! I was going to build a nest too, but then Lauren saw a big boulder over by a tree near the stream and called us over to it. We all climbed up on top of the giant rock, and as we sat there, I saw a bee, lazy and slow, dance around, then land next to my hand. Any other time I would have yelped and tried to shoo it away, or run from it myself. But this bee seemed to be trying to tell me something. His hind end with the yellow and black stripes seemed to be wiggling in a strange rhythm, and I felt as though I was connected to this bee, that he had a message for me that only I could decipher because he spoke a language of bee dancing that only I could understand. I called Lauren over, and she watched the bee dance with me.

I just read what I wrote, and it sounds like a CRAZY person has hijacked this journal, but that's EXACTLY WHAT IT WAS LIKE! It was like the bee and I were TALKING to each other until eventually he flew straight up into the blue, and when he did, I followed him with my eyes, and WOW! The bright blue was dripping down out of the sky and landing with big silver splats onto the grass at the top of the next hill. I told Blake that I had to go see the sky waterfall, and he giggled like a little boy. Then I jumped down off of the Bee Boulder and led the charge up the hill in front of us, chasing the shadow of a cloud up the hill.

At the top of the hill I found myself back at the stream, and just as I turned around, 2 horses came walking up the hill, and I clapped my hand over my mouth and felt shivers of pure joy shooting up and down my spine. It gave me goose bumps all over. Suddenly Blake was at my elbow, and he whispered, C'mon. Then, very slowly, he walked up to one of the horses and held out his hand. The horse snorted and eyed us, then came closer and sniffed his hand, then licked it. Blake told me I had to feel that, and so I held out my hand too. The horse was so powerful, and muscular. It looked like it could just crush us both if it wanted to, but it was kind, and gentle, and when it licked my hand, its tongue felt like warm, wet sandpaper scraping over my palm. It felt AMAZING.

The whole day was like that. I wish I could do it justice as I'm writing about it. I feel like I could use all of the words that I have in my head 100 times each and never be able to tell exactly what it was like. There were so many amazing parts: sitting on the low branch of a big sycamore tree with Blake, and holding hands and talking about the way the sky looked. Then we were just quiet, and I saw sunbeams shimmering out from the edges of a giant cloud, and I felt for sure it was God sending me a signal—a signal that everything was going to be okay; that we were all connected: me, Blake, Lauren, Ian, Ross, the bee, the trees, the horses, the grass, the hills, the whole earth, and everyone on it.

Ross and Lauren and I lay on our backs in the grass and stared up through the leaves of a tree at the blue sky, and the leaves made a canopy that would snap into a grid, then swirl and snap into a grid again. Ross said it was like we were plugged into a big computer program, and Lauren said she thought maybe the acid allowed us to see the way the whole universe really worked. Then she said that she felt so peaceful and safe, and that she loved me and Ross so much, and we said we felt the same way.

Eventually the sun started to sink in the sky, and we started to come down. We walked back to the SUV parked under the tree and sat in it for a while, talking about everything we had seen and experienced, and eating the sandwiches my mom had packed for us.

I wonder how I could possibly explain it to my mom. I mean, I know I couldn't. But it was AMAZING! I wish that she could see it for herself, and Cam and Dad.

By the time we drove home, the sun had set, but it wasn't quite dark yet. I was leaning against Blake in the backseat, and he just held me close and kissed my ear from time to time. My head started to hurt a little, and he told all of us that we'd probably have a headache, so to be sure to drink plenty of water and take some Advil when we got home.

I'd promised Mom that I would be back for dinner at 8 p.m., and it was almost that time when we got back to Blake's, so I called her and told her I would be a few minutes late. She thanked me for letting her know and said she was glad I'd had a good time. Blake walked me over to Lauren's car. He told me he'd be out of town for 6 weeks because he was going to tour the East Coast with his band. UGH! 6 WEEKS???.

They have shows at small clubs in New York, and 2 weeks of rehearsal, then some shows in Boston, then they're going down to Florida and working their way back up to New York and

Toronto. They're playing little clubs, mainly, and opening for a couple of bigger bands. He told me that he'll be really busy, but that when he comes back, he wants to see me.

Then he kissed me again. Maybe it was the leftover acid in my system, or just him—I couldn't tell—but his lips on my mouth were almost electric, and I wrapped both of my arms around his neck and pulled his face into mine.

Lauren and I were quiet as we drove back toward my place, but it was a good, tired quiet. It was a comfortable quiet. The kind of quiet where neither one of you has to say anything because you can almost tell what the other one is thinking. When we pulled into my driveway, I smiled at her, and she reached over and hugged me.

I told her thank you for setting this all up.

She smiled back and said, It's a trip I'll always remember.

August 17

Blake leaves on tour tomorrow. I know he's busy, but he hasn't been texting as much. It makes me feel strange because I felt like we really had a connection last Saturday. Was it just the acid? Was it just because we were tripping? Does Blake text other girls the way he's texting me? I know he's always going to parties and stuff. I'd ask Lauren about it, but I sort of don't want to know for sure. It makes me feel so sad and upset when

I think about it too much. If I don't hear from him tomorrow, maybe I'll call him and see if he picks up.

August 18

BLAKE CALLED ME! I didn't even have to call him. He told me he was sorry that he hadn't texted as much 'cause he'd been rehearsing like 24/7. I told him "good luck" on the tour, and he said he didn't need luck because all he had to do was think about kissing me, and he kicked ass on stage.

Still, 6 weeks feels like an ETERNITY. It'll be OCTOBER when he's back in town. Ugh. Lauren says she's going to keep me distracted. It's going to have to be some pretty major distraction.

August 27

I was just reading over that last entry about Blake from last week, and I was right: Gradually, over the past week his text messages have gotten further and further apart. Although he still sends me a few from time to time. It's weird. Usually they come in the middle of the night.

ANYWAY!

Lauren has been very good about keeping me distracted! I've been having such a great time with her and Ross and Cam. We've been going to the beach a lot—trying to use up as much summer sun as we can before school starts again. Cam comes after he's done with soccer practice or cleaning pools.

Tonight is the last Sunday night before school starts, and Mom and Dad let me have Ross and Lauren over for dinner. Ian came by too. It was funny, because I don't think that Mom realized Ross was dating Ian for a little while. After dinner, Mom and Dad said they'd do the dishes, so Cam and I walked down to the beach with Ross, Ian, and Lauren to watch the sunset. Ross and Ian both had joints, and we passed them around and got a little stoned.

I just sat there thinking about how badly this summer started out and how AWESOME it has ended. I feel like I've got this great circle of friends, and for the first time in my whole life, I feel like I'm making my own decisions.

I watched the sun sink into the waves on the beach, and the colors were so bright and intense. I think pot actually makes sunsets more vibrant somehow. I mean, you're looking at the same colors, but the colors seem to MEAN more. Does that make sense? I mean, who am I asking? My journal? HA HA HA HA HA. I think I may be a little stoned still.

So we're sitting there and Ross put his arm around my shoulders, and I actually got a little teary-eyed. Lauren and Ian were laughing at this story Cam was telling about accidentally knocking one of his customer's cats into their pool with the end of the net and having to fish the cat out of the pool, so they didn't notice, but Ross did.

He asked if I was okay.

I smiled at him and nodded and said, Ross, I'm better than ever.

He smiled at me and kissed me on the cheek, and the two of us just sat there listening to our friends laugh and the waves on the beach, watching the colors in the sky as they became almost unbearably beautiful, and then, like someone had flipped a switch, the sun dropped under the horizon.

I feel like I'm not able to write it down in a way that describes it well enough. There's no way to explain what it feels like to be high, and happy, and held by your good friend as you watch the sun set.

August 28

School starts tomorrow.

Ugh.

I'm going to be a junior.

At least Lauren and Ross and Cam will be there. Mom took the day off work today, and she took Lauren and me school shopping. I've decided that all clothes should have to go through a rite of passage and be tried on by Lauren first.

It's just not FAIR. She's SO pretty. And she has such good

taste. She pulled out all of these really cute jeans that I wouldn't have looked at twice, and FORCED me to try them on. And you know what? She was right. I looked GREAT in them. Mom is always talking about how hard it is to buy me jeans because I'm so picky. She was so relieved that I liked them that she bought three pairs in three different washes. SCORE!

Lauren and Ross are going to meet me and Cam out front in the morning so that Cam can show Lauren around and I can show Ross around. I'm so nervous, I'm not sure how I'm going to fall asleep.

Well, here goes nothing.

August 30

Well, that was one for the BOOKS.

First of all, never underestimate walking into the first day of school with the hot new guy. (Even if he's gay.) It was like, all of a sudden people who had NEVER seen me before suddenly knew my name. Every single girl in every single one of my classes could not take her eyes off Ross. Elizabeth Archer made a beeline for us in her blue-and-gold cheerleader uniform as we walked into first period. Before Mr. Sanders had even finished taking role, she'd passed me a note that read: "Are you going out with Ross?" I almost started giggling. I mean, it's SO predictable. But Elizabeth is sweet. I leaned over and caught her eye and shook my head with a smile. Ross almost wet his pants, he was laughing so hard after class.

The next period Elizabeth made sure to sit down on the other side of Ross. Before the bell rang, she asked him if he had a girlfriend. He whispered, I play for the other team. Elizabeth nodded with that sweet blank look that just showed she had no idea what that meant, then frowned as she looked down at her books, like she was trying to figure out which sport Ross was talking about.

We all got passes to be able to go off campus for lunch, so at 12:35, when the bell rang, Ross and I headed out front to regroup with Cam and Lauren. When we walked out the front door, they were already there, talking with a girl who had light reddish hair—sort of strawberry blond. Cam saw us and waved, and the girl turned around.

It was ASTRID.

You could've knocked me over with a text message. I couldn't BELIEVE it.

All of a sudden the butterflies in my stomach were back. I remembered that at the party, where she and Nathan had materialized out of thin air, she'd said she was transferring schools, but I'd never thought about her coming HERE.

I thought I might have to throw up, but right at that second Ross leaned into me and whispered, It'll be cool. Then he sort of propelled us over to where the three of them were standing.

I could hardly think as we all stood there deciding where to go eat. Finally, as we were walking around the corner to grab sandwiches, Lauren fell in next to me and said, Okay, what's going on? I felt my stomach drop even more, because she could tell just from my face that something was up. She knew about the thing with Nate, but when I told her that Astrid was his girlfriend, her eyes went wide, and she whispered, WOW!

It wound up being okay, though, because at lunch Astrid and Cam were talking and Astrid mentioned that she had just broken up with her boyfriend. Ross and Lauren both shot me a look. I said, You broke up with Nate? I must've sounded like I thought she was crazy, because Lauren and Ross both kicked me under the table, but I DID think she was crazy. I mean who breaks up with a guy like that?

Astrid just smiled at me and said that it was too hard with their different schedules and schools. She said they were still friends and that the good part was Nate would let us know about UCLA parties. Cam jumped in and said that speaking of parties, Jason was planning a big blowout at his house on Labor Day—the last pool party of the summer.

Astrid said thanks for the invite but her parents were having friends over and she was supposed to be there. Cam made his puppy-dog eyes at her, and begged, literally begged her to come to the party. Astrid just smiled and said she'd see what she could do.

Later, when we got back to school, Astrid came to the bathroom with Lauren and me. As we were leaning in to the mirrors surveying the damage of the morning and touching things up, Astrid smiled slyly and said, I can't wait for that Labor Day party. I asked her if she was really coming, and she said of course. Lauren just started giggling. Astrid said she couldn't make it seem like she was TOO eager to go to the party with Cam or else he wouldn't have to work for it. I said, So you like him? And she just put her finger to her lips and winked. When Lauren and I were walking to our lockers, she told me I couldn't say a word; she said it was called playing hard to get and that I should pay attention because it was a necessary skill.

I asked her who in the world was trying to get me.

She raised an eyebrow and said, I think there's a certain up-and-coming rock 'n' roller who has been trying to get in touch with you, isn't there?

I thought about the texts from Blake. They'd sort of petered out. I told her I hadn't heard from him in a while. Lauren laughed and said, See? You're playing so hard to get he's leaving you alone. You know more about this game than you think you do.

Sometimes I think Cam is right. Girls ARE weird.

September 1

AP classes are KILLING me.

ARGH.

Luckily, Lauren and Astrid have chemistry with me, so we get to study together. They were both over tonight so that we could study for our quiz tomorrow. (What kind of sadistic teacher gives a quiz on 40 pages of reading on the FIRST FRIDAY of the school year?)

Anyway, we studied the periodic chart until our brains started to melt, and then I went downstairs to grab us all Diet Cokes. When I got back up to my room, Lauren said she thought chemistry would probably be more enjoyable with a shaker of cosmos.

Astrid asked if there would be booze at Jason's party on Monday because she was pretty sure she was going to have to be a little buzzed to be in a swimsuit in front of Cam and Jason. Lauren laughed and said she would bring a bottle of her dad's vodka just to be sure we could have cosmos. That girl is convinced that it's not a party unless there are cosmos. I said I would make sure that Ross was there with enough pot to smoke us all out. Astrid smiled and said she just might be able to wear her bikini.

Lauren raised her Diet Coke can and said that she was calling for a pledge: a couple hits of weed and cosmos–only school year.

And only on weekends. We all clinked cans in solidarity. Lauren said she'd seen some of the girls at her old school in New York go crazy on REAL drugs like cocaine and stuff. Astrid said that the white drug groups really scared her. I said I'd never even SEEN cocaine before we were at Blake's that one night.

It felt good to have agreed between us that we weren't going to become total party-heads. The girls just left, and I wanted to write this down because I feel so good about having my own group to run with. I've never really been that friendly with other girls before, because I could never predict whether or not they'd be friendly back. The dumb thing is that all that did was ensure that I didn't have any friends at all.

I can't wait for this party on Monday—but I'm also a little nervous. I always get nervous when I'm supposed to be in a bathing suit, and this is definitely a pool party at Jason's. I wish I had Lauren's boobs. Or was as tall and thin as Astrid. SIGH. Oh well. I'll have to get Lauren to help me pick out what I should wear.

September 2

Thank God it's Friday. I survived the chemistry quiz today. BARELY. It's a good thing we all studied last night. The SUPER FUN part is that Lauren and I both decided to audition for the choir and we BOTH GOT IN! She's an alto and I'm a soprano.

The bad news: When I came home, Mom made me help her fold laundry and dust and vacuum my room. Ugh. I HATE not having a housekeeper. Mom and Dad decided that we should Tighten Our Collective Belt and just have Maria come in to clean on special occasions, not once a week like we used to. I know that sounds bratty. I'm lucky that we can afford to have a nice house near the ocean. I guess the least I can do is clean my own room.

The good news: Cam just got home from soccer practice, and we're going to meet Ross and Lauren for a movie up on the Promenade. He told me that he asked Astrid if she wanted to come earlier, but she hasn't called him back or texted him one way or the other. I texted Ross to make sure that he brought some of the GREEN drug group as Astrid would call it. It will be fun to see a movie stoned! I've never done that before!

September 3

Last night was a bummer. Ross couldn't get in touch with Ian until later, so he didn't have any pot. It was still fun to hang out with everyone, but it would've been SO COOL to get stoned and see a movie. Oh well. It's not like the end of my world. I got sort of upset in the moment when I found out that Ross didn't have any, but I kept it to myself. I didn't want to seem like THAT girl, like a big whiner who couldn't have fun unless she had pot.

After the movie Cam went over to Jason's because they've got soccer practice tomorrow morning. The big homecoming game is in a few weeks. I didn't have to be home until midnight, so Ross and I went to Lauren's place. Her dad was there, and I met him. He's a nice guy, but we couldn't have cosmos then either. BUMMER.

Ross went out on the balcony to smoke a cigarette and Lauren and I went with him. While we were out there, his phone rang and it was Ian. After they talked, Ross hung up and was sort of quiet. Lauren asked him what was up, and Ross said he didn't really want to talk about it. I asked him if everything was okay with him and Ian, and Ross just laughed and said that even if it weren't, there were plenty of other guys. Lauren grabbed my phone to take a picture of me and Ross on the balcony, and after she did, a text message popped up while she was holding it and Lauren saw that it was from BLAKE.

She and Ross were both ON IT. They made me show them all of the texts from Blake and they were hooting and laughing so loudly that Lauren's dad came out onto the balcony to ask if everything was okay. My face was BEET RED. I was SO embarrassed.

Ross said that he wished he had a guy as cute as Blake banging his door down. Lauren asked me why I was so embarrassed. She said that this was totally a good thing. I just told her that I didn't know, but I always got so nervous around guys. Especially guys like Blake. The only time I've ever been brave around a guy was the night of my birthday with Nate, and that was a craptastic failure.

Then Lauren reminded me of the night at Blake's on the diving board, and I remembered how uninhibited I'd felt dancing with her. She also said I looked pretty at ease that day we all went hiking. I said, Yeah, but I don't want to have to drink until I hurl, or drop acid every time I want to feel comfortable with a guy. Ross agreed that was a good idea. (The not drinking till I barf/dropping acid part.)

Lauren said it was no problem. She has a prescription for something called Xanax that she got from a psychiatrist in New York. (I had to google how to spell it. I thought it started with a Z, like it sounds. Who knew?) Ross and I were just blinking at her, and she rolled her eyes and explained that it was no big deal, that he'd prescribed it because she was really anxious about her mom's boyfriend being a jerk to her.

We went back inside and up to her bedroom. She dug a bottle out of her purse and took out a tiny white pill that was like a rectangular bar. She broke two little parts off of the bar and gave one to Ross and one to me. She said we should take them before the party on Monday and we'd feel as relaxed as ever. EVEN if there were cute boys around.

I put the little pill in the small pocket of my jeans. When I got home just now, I slipped it into the bottle with my allergy medicine that I take sometimes.

Now I'm not nervous about the party on Monday at ALL. Somehow just knowing I have a pill to try makes me feel really excited about the party—but not worried excited, just FUN excited!

September 5

I have to get in bed right now. But I just wanted to write and say that we had a BLAST at the Labor Day party today. Astrid showed up and Cam almost had a heart attack. Jason's parents were in Las Vegas for Labor Day, so there were about 50 kids there from school. Ian showed up for a bit to hang with Ross.

That Xanax Lauren gave me made me feel loopy, but calm. It wasn't like smoking pot. It was less in my head and more in my body somehow. It was different because I didn't feel like I was underwater, the way that pot sometimes makes me feel— like I'm moving through Jell-O. This was different. It was slight, but it just took the edge off. It was like falling backward onto a really puffy pile of pillows.

HA HA HA HA HA HA

I think that's enough. RIDICULOUS. I must still be feeling it. I just felt really happy. It didn't even bother me that Lauren couldn't find any vodka there. I didn't even feel like drinking at the party. Cam had a couple of beers with Jason, and there were a couple of girls from school who drank so much beer that they threw up in the azaleas in the corner of Jason's backyard.

Anyway, I was wearing a little red bikini Lauren loaned me, and I felt like I could talk to anybody I wanted to. This guy named Mark who is in my English class came up and started talking to me. He's tall, and really cute, and on the football team, but he's also really smart. He won some sort of academic award last year. I've always noticed him, but he's one of those guys I would never just walk up and talk to. And HE came up and talked to ME! He saw that Lauren and I were just drinking Diet Coke and said something about how he didn't drink, and it was nice to see that there were girls at the party who weren't on anything either.

I just looked at Lauren. I saw her raise her eyebrows behind her big black Chanel sunglasses. I decided not to say anything. He didn't need to know that we'd taken Xanax. He's got this really cute dimple when he smiles. He told me he'd see me in class tomorrow. I felt this really warm feeling in my stomach about this Mark guy. He's the kind of guy my mom would be THRILLED about me bringing home for dinner.

On the way home, Lauren told Ross that he wouldn't have believed how chatty I was with Mark. Ross gave me a high five. Of course then Blake texted me again. Lauren asked me how long I was gonna string that poor boy along.

I'd never admit it to anyone, but it's kind of fun knowing that there's this 20-year-old guy who can't stop thinking about me!

September 6

Not much went on today.

Had choir with Lauren.

Lunch with Lauren and Astrid in the CRAPateria. Ross was out sick. Cam went off campus with Jason and a bunch of the soccer players.

Mark is in choir. He's a baritone. How did I never notice him before? He smiled at me today. I thought about going up to talk to him, but then I saw a picture of me in that red bikini on Facebook. UNTAG. It was a nightmare. I look weird, like my proportions aren't right. Lauren has these perfect long limbs, and I just looked skinny fat. I only ate half of my dinner tonight. Mom asked if I was feeling well. I said I was fine.

I wish I could sing more. When I'm singing and we're all following Mr. Brown and I hear the harmony with all of the other voices, I forget everything else. Or, not forget, but I can't think about anything else—just listening and singing the right notes.

September 8

Things get so boring so fast. I've got all this reading to do for AP English. I'm like 20 pages into THE GRAPES OF WRATH and I can barely keep my eyes open.

I can't even hang out with Ross while I do it because he always has the bright idea to get stoned and then read. Of course, we read for like 27 seconds and then sit around giggling and talking instead of actually reading. Yesterday we tried it, and he wound up painting his toenails green with this old nail polish he found in my bathroom. He's hilarious.

I just remembered HOMECOMING is at the end of the month. I'M SAVED! It's so much more fun when there's something to look forward to. Maybe I'll see if we can all figure out a place to have a party after the dance!

September 10

Tomorrow is a Sunday, and in the afternoon our choir from school is singing at a concert the city is hosting to commemorate the 9/11 attacks. I was so little when 9/11 happened; I just remember that Mom didn't go to work, and she kept Cam and me home from school, but we weren't allowed to watch TV. She put on a couple of movies for us, and when Dad came home, I remember that he and Mom were so quiet.

Now that I'm older, I've looked up the footage online of the planes hitting the buildings, and I can sort of understand why Mom didn't want Cam and me to see that when we were so little. I don't really understand it. It's like watching a movie.

I asked Lauren what it was like, actually being there in New York. She said that they were running late that morning and her mom was just dropping her off at school when the first plane hit the towers. She said that they could see this giant black plume of smoke coming from downtown, and her mom told her they were going back home. Her dad had a group of 8 friends who played poker together. Three of them worked in the towers. Two of them were killed. The 3rd one had called in sick that day.

Lauren still thinks that her dad and mom got divorced because of September 11. I asked her if it was because her dad was sad about his friends. She shook her head. She said she thinks it's because they weren't happy and 9/11 made them realize how short life was. She said they were divorced a year later.

That makes me sad to think about. I mean, not just all the people who died but that Lauren had to be so sad because her dad left, and then going through all those years of having her mom's new boyfriend hit on her.

That makes me so damn mad.

September 12

Today at school Mark followed Lauren and me to our lockers after choir. Then he asked me if I wanted to go to the homecoming dance with him. Right there! In front of Lauren, and the whole wide world. I was like, um . . . and Lauren closed her locker and said, Mark, you seem like a good guy. If you don't mind can I offer you some advice?

Then without waiting for him to say anything, she smiled and told him that probably there was a smoother way to ask someone to homecoming than a hallway ambush and that maybe he'd like to regroup and see if he could come up with some other way to catch my attention than just a surprise attack after 6th period. The whole time she was saying this she was opening a little spiral notebook that she always carries in her purse and scribbling something on a page, then she tore it out and handed it to him. She told him this was my phone number and that if he wanted to ask me out, he might try just calling first and seeing if I was interested in talking.

Then she grabbed my hand, told me to close my mouth, (which was hanging open), and then dragged me down the hall and out to the parking lot.

I'm glad she told me to close my mouth so I didn't trip over my lips.

We got into her car, and I just started laughing. I couldn't believe she did that for me. Astrid and Ross got into the car with us, and Lauren filled them in on what had just happened. I wasn't sure if I wanted to go to homecoming with Mark or not, but I sure didn't want to have to answer him right that second.

Lauren drove us around the block while Ross packed a bowl and passed the pipe around, and we all weighed the pros and cons of Mark Wilson. Lauren said that he is very cute but we hardly know him, and I agreed. Ross told me he thought I was crazy for turning down a guy that hot, and if I didn't go with Mark, he might try to. We all laughed about that, and Astrid didn't see what the problem was with saying yes. I told her I wanted to have a little party after homecoming and didn't want him to freak out if we smoked or had a couple of drinks. He'd made such a big deal about how great it was that Lauren and I weren't drinking at the Labor Day party, so I had a sneaking suspicion that he'd have a problem with dating a girl who did.

The pot helped me calm down a little. My heart stopped racing, and when I got home I ate half a bag of carrot sticks. I swear, if I give in to the munchies every time I get high I'm going to weigh 400 pounds by the time I'm a senior. Now I'm tired. I'm going to take a nap so that I can stay awake to finish GRAPES OF WRATH.

Later . . .

Mark just called while I was sleeping and left a voice mail. I don't know what to do. I am not really sure I want to go to homecoming with him, but at the same time I'm not sure I'm in a position to be turning down dates offered by cute, nice guys.

Do I just want to go with someone else so that I can party a little? Could I have fun with Mark and just stay sober? When I think about that, I get all disappointed and sad thinking about Ross and Lauren and Astrid and Cam having fun and me not.

OMG. I just wrote that if I couldn't drink or smoke pot I wouldn't have any fun. Do I really think that?

Now Lauren's calling me. Stand by.

Later . . .

Lauren is SO FUNNY. She's already found us dates who don't mind if we drink. LOL. She said I can go out with Mark whenever I want, but to tell him that I already have a date for homecoming. Lauren said there are these two senior guys named Andrew and Ryan in her British literature class who keep trying to ask her out. She said they're best friends and have this competition going to see who she'll go out with first. She called Andrew and told him that we would go to homecoming with him and Ryan just as friends. She said it's better anyway because now I'm playing hard to get for Mark.

I asked her if I was Ryan's date or Andrew's date. She just laughed and said, Oh c'mon. Who cares? Take your pick.

Ross just texted me: IF YOU BREAK THAT BOY'S HEART I'LL BE HAPPY TO BE THE SHOULDER HE CAN CRY ON.

LOL. I love my friends.

September 13
Told Mark today that I already had a date for homecoming but that we could go see a movie or something if he wanted. He was a little disappointed, but he smiled and that dimple of his poked in. He said that would be great. We made a plan to go and see that new superhero movie when it opens this weekend.

September 14
Astrid and Lauren had to rescue me from Cam a second ago. JEEEZ. I'm so glad I have a free period now so I can write about it. I was just at lunch in the cafeteria with Astrid and Lauren and Ross when Cam came marching over and said that he'd been in the locker room for PE and heard Ryan and

Andrew talking about this hot junior chick they were taking to homecoming with the new girl, and about how they were going to get me drunk and see how far they could go with me.

Ross started laughing and Cam slammed his hand down on the table and was like IT'S NOT FUNNY.

Lauren told him that he needed to take a big deep breath. Cam told her that she needed to back off, that I was his little sister and he was taking care of me. I stood up and told him to shut up, that he was embarrassing me and I could take care of myself.

He looked around and saw that everybody was staring at us. Astrid grabbed his hand and pulled him down next to her. He got quiet, but his eyes were still bright and angry.

Lauren told him that we were all just going as friends. She said, Besides, your sis has a hot date with Mark Wilson this weekend. You certainly can't object to that, can you?

Cam asked me if that was true. I nodded, and he smiled really big and said, That's awesome sis!

I swear, Cam can go from hot to cold and back in 12 seconds flat.

All I can think about is that two senior guys called me THIS HOT JUNIOR CHICK.

OMG! SENIORS THINK I'M HOT!

I know. I know. I'm supposed to not be excited about that.

Sue me. I don't see my brains when I look in the mirror. It wasn't the A on my GRAPES OF WRATH report that made Mark Wilson want to ask me to homecoming.

September 15

Mark Wilson is following me and Lauren and Astrid around like a puppy dog. Who knew telling a boy to cool his jets could be so effective? Today Lauren invited Ryan and Andrew to come to lunch with us, only I didn't know it. So, when I walked out front, there they were with her and Astrid. Of course, Mark had followed me outside and had just started to ask me to lunch when Lauren saw me and waved me over.

I smiled at Mark and asked him what time he was picking me up tomorrow night for the movie. He stared at Ryan (who was smirking at me) and Andrew (who was trying to pinch Lauren's butt until she smacked him) and looked like he'd just swallowed a golf ball.

He said 7. I said, make it 6:45 so you have time to meet my parents.

Then I turned around and walked to lunch with Lauren and the boys without looking back.

But my heart was totally racing! I could feel Mark staring after me. I felt so powerful!

I think Lauren is right: This is making Mark crazy hot for me.

September 16

Mark will be here any minute. I borrowed this little black skirt from Lauren that makes my legs look 27 miles long. He's not going to know what hit him.

OMG! I've NEVER felt like this before a date. Last year when Sean took me to homecoming, I was so nervous I threw up while I was doing my makeup.

I'm not even worried about this now. I mean, I know I don't look as good as Lauren or anything, but this boy is whipped for me. I wonder if I'll kiss him tonight?

Hmmmmmm. Maybe I'll make him suffer. HA HA HA HA HA. I'm so bad.

Oooh! That's him. Here goes nothing!

(I'll report back as soon as I'm home.)

September 17

Okay, the movie was SO LAAAAAAAAAAME. Superheroes who just magically win everything in the end are SO BORING.

And that was the BEST part of the evening. I mean, Mark is so sweet, but he's so . . . SERIOUS. After the movie, we went to get ice cream on the Promenade, and while we were eating, he told me all about how worried he was about me going out with Ryan for homecoming. He said that Ryan only had one thing on the brain, and it wasn't honorable.

Honorable.

Who uses that word?

I totally played stupid, and was like, What does Ryan have on his brain that isn't honorable, Mark? (Wide eyes, blinking, blank look, the whole nine.) Then I crossed my incredibly bare legs and tugged at Lauren's little black skirt. (Also, I cannot BELIEVE my mother let me out of the house in it. I saw the look on her face when I walked down the stairs, but then she met Mark and probably knew she had nothing to worry about.)

ANYWAY, Mark then spent like 20 MINUTES showing me this necklace he wears with a little key on it, and how it's part of this pledge he made at his church. Apparently, the key is the key to his "heart" and he's not supposed to unlock it until his wedding night with the woman who is going to be his wife.

I mean, WHAT? I get it that I am young and shouldn't just throw myself at the first guy I see. I'm a virgin, and I do want my first time to be special with someone who I really care about. But I have this idea that I'm going to probably have a boyfriend at some point before I get married who I'll want to sleep with. I'll use condoms and all of that; I'm not stupid.

But Mark was SERIOUS. I was like, Hold up. A big handsome guy like you is a VIRGIN? And then I sort of smiled, and he saw it and said, Are you making fun of me? And I giggled, and said, No. No, I'm not. But I couldn't stop smiling.

And then he started smiling because I was smiling and then we were both laughing, and he said, What?

I didn't say anything, I just got up and grabbed his hand and led him out toward the parking deck and his car. I held his hand while he opened the car door for me, and when we got in, I leaned over to kiss him. He actually put his hand on my shoulder and held me back.

Then he asked me what I was doing!

I said, What does it look like I'm doing? Is this a trick question?

He told me that he didn't want us to go too fast on our first date.

I almost busted out laughing right in front of him, but I just smiled really big and nearly chewed a hole on the inside of my cheek to keep from giggling. When he saw my smile, he sat back in the driver's seat and let out a big, relieved sigh, then took my hand and told me that he was so happy that I was smiling because he could tell I understood and felt the same way.

I was almost crying from holding back the laughter. All I could think about was winding up practically naked in Blake's bathroom that first night I met him, and how poor Mark would have a meltdown if he knew about that. I'm afraid all the circuits in his brain might melt and then he'd never be able to unlock his heart with that little key around his neck.

The minute he dropped me off I called Lauren and was like, OMG! Come. Over. NOW.

Mom was very pleased that I was a.) home early from my date, b.) that Lauren came over and wanted to hang out at our place. (She worries that Lauren spends so much time alone because her mom is in New York.) Mom made us popcorn and then went to bed. Lauren and I went up to my room to watch movies and Lauren had a surprise. She'd brought a pill for us to split. She said it was a muscle relaxer and gave me half. I asked her what it did, and she said, Just mellows you out.

That little pill was AWESOME. In my body, it was like I'd smoked pot, only my head wasn't cloudy at ALL. It wasn't like being drunk. I just wanted to lie really still, and it felt like I was melting into the bed, but I wasn't tired.

When I told Lauren all about Mark, she laughed her ass off—especially the part about his necklace and saving it to open up his heart for his wife on his wedding night.

I feel sort of bad writing that. I mean, Mark is very sweet. I don't want to make fun of him, but it's just FUNNY.

Anyway, I slipped off to sleep at some point and slept like a rock. Usually it's hard to sleep in my bed if somebody spends the night, but not with that little yellow pill we took. It was like I was sleeping on a cloud in a deep dark cave.

This morning Lauren went home to write a paper she has due for her British literature class.

It's a good thing we're both very together. See, All Adults Everywhere? Not all teenagers who swallow pills and smoke pot die in car accidents. Some of us are very responsible!

September 18

Nothing much.

Ross was going to come over today and have dinner with us, but his grandma is in town from Boca Raton, so he's eating at the hotel with his mom.

I'm all done with my homework.

I was bored and messing around on my phone, and I read a bunch of the texts that Blake had sent me. I haven't heard from him much since he left on tour. I felt sort of nervous when I thought about texting him. He's probably got girls in every town swarming all over him. But I texted him anyway, just to say hi. He texted me back like IMMEDIATELY. And it wasn't a sex text either. He just said: HOW ARE YOU BEAUTIFUL?

OH! THE BIG NEWS: Cam asked Astrid to homecoming. It's so weird that my friend thinks my brother is cute. EW. I mean, he's a nice guy, and I guess Cam is cute and everything, but I just keep thinking about what a pain in

the neck he is sometimes and how he picks his nose in the car
when he thinks no one is looking.

EW.

September 20

Ross told us today that Ian invited us all up to his parents'
house in the Hollywood Hills after homecoming to hang and
use the hot tub and stuff. Ian's dad is some big movie producer
and he's scouting locations in Italy until Christmas. Anyway,
Ian's got their big place to himself, and we're all invited. Astrid
and Lauren and I are going shopping for outfits tonight.
Homecoming is a pretty casual thing, so Mom put me on a
strict budget: $50 toward an outfit. I told her that $50 MIGHT
buy me one sleeve of a top. She said that maybe I'd remember
this when I got Christmas money from Gramps this year. I told
her maybe I'd just have to go topless.

She said that she'd be happy to give me just $25 if that
would make me stop whining.

GOD!

I guess I should be glad that I'm getting anything at all.
Dad just looked at me and said that I should be grateful. It's
not that I'm not grateful; I just know that Lauren and Astrid
will have all-new outfits that will make them look like a
kabillion dollars.

Anyway, Astrid said she'd help me pick out stuff that would work, and Lauren said I could raid her closet for stuff. That'll be good because she has SO. MANY. SHOES!

September 22

Tomorrow is homecoming. It's going to be so much fun!

Ryan and Andrew actually took Lauren and me to lunch today. It was sorta sweet. Although, Ryan talks about himself a LOT. It's not so bad, but it just gets kind of boring. I saw Mark watching me as I walked down the hall with Ryan and Andrew. I smiled and raised my hand in a little wave, and he just shook his head and turned around. I wonder who he's going to go to homecoming with? He hadn't asked anybody last week when we went on our date.

Anyway, at lunch Ryan would NOT shut up about this point he scored in their beach volleyball game last week and how TOTALLY RADICAL the spike had been, and how Andrew had given him the assist. Apparently, they play every weekend down at the beach and won a 2-on-2 tournament.

Lauren rolled her eyes and interrupted him at one point and said, So, Andy, do you often assist Ryan with his balls?

They both acted all hurt and were like NO WAY, that's cold. Lauren said that it wasn't as cold as she would be if she had to fight to get a word in edgewise all night tomorrow night.

I just started laughing and told Ryan that I live right up the street from the beach. He smiled at me all bashful, like he was secretly pleased, and said that I should come check out a match sometime. I said that maybe I'd bring Cam down with me next weekend if things went well at homecoming. It effectively reminded them that Cam is indeed my brother, and that sort of shut both of them up for a second. Cam is probably a head taller than both of them and has bigger muscles, too.

While we were shopping on Wednesday night, Astrid told me and Lauren that Cam and Jason had tossed both of them up against the lockers and threatened to brain them if either one of them caused us any trouble at lunch or at homecoming. I actually don't mind that Cam is being so protective. Ryan seems nice enough. He actually held the door for me today, but I don't really know him.

Mom says that's what a date is all about: getting to know someone. Of course, she wants to get to know them first, so she made me introduce them to her last weekend after Cam's game.

I dunno. Maybe I'm just a dumb girl, but there is something about boys after a soccer game when they're all sweaty and gross that makes me think they're really hot. Mark walked up to say hi to my parents while we were all talking to Ryan and Andrew, and he looked really good, even though he smelled pretty bad. Of course, Mom and Dad were all smiley and like HI MARK!

as if he was their long-lost son or something. Ryan just looked at me like What. Is. Up?

AWK-WARD.

Anyway, Elizabeth Archer is our junior class princess on the homecoming court, naturally, although Ross said it shoulda been this kid in our chemistry class named Raymond. Raymond is SO QUEENY. All the girls think it's kinda funny in a cute way, but the older guys pick on him a lot, Andrew especially. Cam has told him to lay off several times, but when you come to school wearing eyeliner, there's only so much Cam can do for you.

Ross is out, at school, but he doesn't act any differently than Cam or Mark, or any of the straight guys. He just looks like a cute surfer. Guys like Raymond have it worse, 'cause they just come across as really different from everyone else. Ross will tell you he's gay if you ask, but he just kind of blends in. Raymond really stands out.

The worst part is that Raymond has this CRAZY CRUSH on Ross. He asked Ross if he wanted to go the homecoming dance, and Ross was kind, but firm. I can tell it bothers Ross that the guys will start picking on him the way they pick on Raymond. Every time Andrew is picking on Raymond, Ross clears out of there as fast as he can.

Anyway, Ian is actually going to come to the homecoming game with Ross, and then we're all going to go to the dance

119

together. I already told Ross that I want to sneak back to the car with him before we go into the dance and smoke a bowl.

OH! And I have to remind Lauren about another little chunk of Xanax.

September 23

Holy. Moses.

Why do they even HAVE school the day of homecoming. It's taking FOR. EV. ER.

And we still have to get through the damn pep rally. Elizabeth Archer is so excited about it, she's about to explode. I am sitting behind her, and she keeps turning around to wink and smile at me and Ross. Elizabeth is wearing the new cheerleading uniforms she and the squad earned washing cars in their bikinis over the summer. The skirts are so short they're almost nonexistent.

Ross asked me if I wanted to get stoned at lunch, but I told him NO. Under no circumstances do we smoke during school. THAT would make us total STONERS.

And we're not stoners.

We smoke in the parking lot AFTER school.

He rolled his eyes, and shook his head.

Then Lauren walked up and said she had a quarter of a Xanax bar for each of us that she'd be handing out right after last period. Ross called her the Fairy Godmother of Pharmaceuticals, and Astrid laughed really hard.

Oh, crap!

Mrs. Winslow just called on me because she saw me writing and thought I was taking notes. I had NO IDEA what she was talking about. I haven't really had to pay attention in a history class in years. Newsflash: American history doesn't change much after 5th grade. Pretty much, you've hit the high points by then.

I better put this away. The last thing I need is for it to get confiscated. Jeez.

I CAN'T WAIT FOR TONIIIIIIIIIGHT!

September 24

I don't even know where to start. I'm in real trouble. Serious. Trouble. Last night was a complete nightmare. I am so scared. I don't even know who to talk to. I want to go tell my mom all about it right this second, but I can't. I'm so afraid that she'll never let me leave the house again. I can't even write about this. I'm crying so hard, I can't see what I'm writing.

Later . . .

Lauren just left. She came over to make me feel better. I love her so much. I know I've only known her for a couple of months, but I don't really remember my life without her. I don't know how I would've made it through the day without her. She gave me another little chunk of Xanax, and I'm finally feeling relaxed for the first time all day.

Mom must think I've lost my mind. She thinks I just had a bad date.

Jeez. That's the understatement of the year.

I'm too tired to even think about writing all of this down now, but I will first thing when I get up tomorrow. I need to write it down. I want to. Something about writing it down will make some sense of what happened last night.

I hope.

September 25

It's Sunday morning. I'm feeling better today. I was just lying here in my bed, and I felt the fear flood into my stomach again, like the fog that hides the sun on June mornings. I know I just have to keep moving this pen across the page, but everything in me says that if I tell the truth about what happened Friday night, that'll make it real somehow, and I don't know if I can even face the memory in my head, much less watch the words come out of the pen and onto the paper in this journal.

It started out easy, and bright. The pep rally was crazy, and then Lauren passed out the Xanax, and Ross, Lauren, Astrid, and I all headed over to Lauren's place to order food and get ready for the dance. Lauren's dad is out of town this weekend, so she mixed us up some cosmos as soon as we got to her place, and by the time we'd had one, the food had arrived and the Xanax had kicked in. We ate and then started getting ready.

We laughed until our mascara ran and we all had to do it again. That's what I mainly remember about getting ready: laughing.

Ross was SO FUNNY. He'd only had one cosmo 'cause they're too girly, but he'd smoked a whole bowl of pot himself, then finished all of our leftovers while we all got ready. He was ready to go in like two minutes. He had a new polo and a pair of skinny jeans that looked like he was melted and poured into them. He lay down in the Jacuzzi tub in Lauren's HUGE bathroom and cracked jokes while he smoked pot and we straightened our hair. Well, Lauren and I straightened; Astrid curled. There were lots of hair ironing devices.

Then finally we were ready and Ross let out a low whistle, and then we spent like 20 minutes taking pictures of each other in various configurations. Of course, then Andrew and Ryan showed up, and they'd brought beer that Andrew had nabbed out of his dad's beer fridge in the garage. Ross smoked them out and had a beer, and the three of them seemed to bond or something. At one point Andrew told Ross he was okay for a homo, and Ross told Andrew that he was not bad for a breeder, and the two of them collapsed on the couch laughing and blowing pot smoke all over the place.

At that point Astrid looked at her watch and herded us all out the door.

For some reason, stepping outside made me realize how hard the Xanax had hit on top of the cosmos. All of a sudden I was floating, but it wasn't as clean as just Xanax or a muscle relaxer. I'd only smoked one hit of pot, but on top of two cosmos and the pill, I was a little foggy, and as we crowded into the elevators at Lauren's condo, I wobbled a little on my heels. I was glad that Ryan had big arms. He smiled at me when I was teetering toward the wall, offered me his arm, and asked if I was okay.

I smiled and said that I was fine. He raised an eyebrow and said, Oh, I can see you're fine. You're the finest girl I've ever taken to a dance; that's for damn sure.

I blushed HARD when he said that. Then Lauren said, God, Andy, your friend RyRy is a total cheese ball.

And then we were laughing again.

Ian joined us in the stands at the game. He looked great, and Ross got that big goofy grin on his face when they sat down together next to me. The crowd was WILD. We all were. The air was crisp and you could smell the ocean from the soccer field. Elizabeth Archer cheered right at Ross during the big halftime routine. Then as the junior class princess she was escorted across the field by Jason. Astrid snickered when she saw this and said that Megan Archer wouldn't give Jason the time of day, so he was escorting Elizabeth to homecoming in hopes of showing up on her radar.

We won the game, and Cam joined us after he had showered and changed. Astrid went walking up to him in her impossibly high heels that made her almost come to his chin. He bent down and kissed her softly on the lips. Ross punched him in the shoulder and said that he didn't care what the two of them did behind closed doors, but he didn't want them flaunting their lifestyle choice in his face, which made Cam laugh so hard he snorted.

We didn't want to be the very first ones at the dance, so we walked to the back of the parking lot and took turns sliding into Ian's gigantic Land Rover to smoke a bowl. Then Lauren dragged me and Astrid into her car so that we could touch up. LAST LOOKS EVERYONE! she yelled. She said that's what they say on movie and music-video sets before they shoot the scene so that the makeup people know to dab powder and fix hair.

When we were in her car, she passed around a silver flask she said her dad keeps in the kitchen and never uses. It was filled with cosmos. Naturally.

Then we headed into the dance.

And we DANCED.

It was hilarious. Ian is SUCH a good dancer, and he's 20, so he doesn't give a crap about what high school kids think of him. Every girl in the place wanted to dance with him, and every guy in the gym wanted to BE him because every girl wanted him, but when there was a slow dance, he pulled Ross in, and held him close, and flipped off anybody who gave him a dirty look.

That's what I want. I want somebody who has my back.

Ryan was an okay dancer, but he was REEEEEALLY stoned and had slammed a couple of beers in the parking lot, so he smelled sort of skunky. Still, it was fun. He kept telling me how sexy I was and how I was making him crazy. He tried to press his junk up against me every 30 seconds, and I just let him. It was fun watching him get all red in the face.

Then I'd drag him over and make him dance with Ross and Ian and me. Lauren did the same thing with Andrew, and by the time we'd been in the gym for an hour, we'd danced ourselves as sweaty as Cam was when he'd walked off the soccer field.

And then we were leaving. Cam and Astrid hadn't moved apart from each other in like an hour, and Ian was trying to take his shirt off, which is against dress code at the dance, and Ross had to drag him out into the parking lot, laughing, and I looked at Lauren, and she said, Let's blow this joint. And I said, A JOINT sounds GREAT!

Lauren went over and tapped on Cam's shoulder. He finally came up for air with Astrid, and he said they'd meet us at Ian's dad's place.

I shoulda gone home right that second.

Crap. Now I'm crying again. And Mom just called up the stairs. We're driving up to have lunch at my grandparents' house. I'll have to finish this in the car.

Later . . .

It's too hard to write while we're driving. I can't tell if it's the butterflies in my stomach or the motion of the car. Either way, it's making me a little sick.

Later . . .

I feel better now that I've eaten. I think I was just hungry. Grams made a big pot roast with all the trimmings. She had this giant yellow cake with fudge frosting, like the ones you see on the commercials for Betty Crocker, only this one didn't come from a mix: She made it from scratch. It's Cam's favorite dessert. I had a very small slice. It was good to see Cam smile again, even if it was about cake. Sometimes he seems so easy. All it took to put him in a good mood again was food.

Cam dragged me into the kitchen with him to do the dishes so that Grams and Gramps could hang out with Mom and Dad

127

for a while. Actually, it was so he could talk to me about what happened at homecoming. At least he's not yelling at me like he did on Friday.

It all happened so fast after we got to Ian's parents' place, which is this HUGE house in the hills. The whole place looks like it might teeter off the side of the hill with one stiff wind and we'd wind up crashing down the hill into the big strip of trendy nightclubs below.

The view took my breath away. You could see downtown to the left and all the way to the edge of city and the beach on the right.

Ian and Ross beat us there because Lauren wanted to stop and get cranberry juice so that we could make cosmos just in case they didn't have the right mixers. Ryan was driving because Andrew was totally tanked. He'd slammed like 3 of the beers he and Ryan brought during the dance. He kept whinnying like a horse and trying to slap Lauren's butt. Lauren was not amused.

When we got to Ian's, she made a beeline for the kitchen to whip up some drinks. Ryan and Andrew followed her inside, and I stopped by the pool to take in the view. There's something about being up in the air like this and seeing the whole city laid out below me that never gets old. It looks beautiful from so far away, like somebody lined up perfect strands of red-and-white holiday lights in a grid and then plugged in the whole city.

When you're driving around down in it, there's so much light, and noise and honking and screaming and laughter and music, but up in the hills, it looks so peaceful and everything is so quiet.

I was thinking about all that when I heard a voice behind me say, Beautiful, isn't it?

I knew it was Blake before I turned around, and before I could, I felt his arms slide around my waist. He pulled me in toward his chest from behind and whispered in my ear:

It's beautiful, like you.

Maybe it was the pot, or the Xanax, or maybe it was just how I felt in the moment, but before I knew what was happening, he had pulled me in and we were kissing! Right in front of everyone.

And I didn't care.

At that same moment Lauren came walking in the door with my drink.

What the hell are you doing?? She said it in a loud whisper that sounded angry, but when I saw her face, she was about to laugh. I stepped away from Blake, blushing.

I couldn't believe Blake had shown up! He said he'd just gotten back last night and Lauren had told him about homecoming tonight and invited him up.

Lauren handed me a cosmo and told me I better watch it because Tweedle Dumb and Tweedle Dumber are in there getting wasted right now and I didn't want to start a brawl by kissing Blake in front of my date.

Blake laughed and said he could handle a coupla high school guys.

That's when we went inside and I saw Ross bending over the mirror on the coffee table in the living room. Then I heard him take a huge sniff and throw his head back and shout, WHOO!

Ian was sitting next to him and kissed him and laughed. Only, it wasn't a normal laugh. It was sort of wild and loud. When he turned around, his eyes were wide and darted back and forth between us. When he saw me and Lauren, he yelled, LADIES!

Blake laughed and led us down two short steps into the living room. He asked us if we wanted any party favors. I looked at Ross and said, WHAT are you DOING? I couldn't believe he was doing coke. I could see that Ryan and Andrew were out on the balcony off of the living room smoking cigarettes.

Ian just laughed and told me to relax, that Ross just did a little bump.

Then, before I knew what had happened, Lauren was bending over the mirror. She came up, sniffed, and tossed her long blond hair over her shoulder. She turned to me and said a single word:

C'mon.

I looked down at the little straight line of powder next to the larger pile. There was a little straw in her hand. My heart started racing faster than the beat of the music.

I glanced over at Blake, who grinned at me and said, You're gonna like it!

I looked around at everyone else. Ian was tickling Ross on the couch. Ryan and Andrew were staring through the window with their cigarettes. I could smell the fingers of smoke tickling my nose through the partially opened door. When they saw me contemplating the mirror, they started chanting, DO IT DO IT DO IT . . .

Something in me knew that this was the only chance. If Cam were here, I'd never do this. But it was so . . . COOL. There was this big house in the hills and a pile of cocaine, and I wouldn't do a lot, just a little bump. Besides, it was an event! Blake was back, and we were all together, and it would just be this one special time.

I took the straw from Lauren.

I smiled up at her as she set the mirror down on the table. I slid in next to Ian and said, Okay! Okay! How do I DO this?

She giggled and said, Just put the straw down and sniff the line up into your nose.

I laughed and started to lean forward, but Blake yelled, WAIT!

I froze and looked up at him like I'd been caught or something.

He looked at me and said, Before you bend over the mirror, make sure you've exhaled so you can inhale through your nose. Otherwise you'll end up exhaling and blowing coke all over the room.

I breathed out.

I touched the edge of the straw to the little line and then put the straw in my nose and sniffed. I saw the white powder disappear up the straw, then felt a little sting in my nose. I dropped the straw and sat back on the couch and sniffed again.

I felt the little clump of powder in my nose hit the back of my throat and make my mouth water with a strange, bitter flavor that made the back of my throat numb.

Ryan and Andrew came into the living room, hooting. Lauren giggled. Ross jumped up, grabbed my hand, and yelled TO THE HOT TUB!

That's when things sped up. I remember the rest in snapshots.

I felt a WHOOSH of something that made me smile and laugh. It was like the first drop on a roller coaster; the excitement flooded my whole body, and I know this sounds completely made up, but I felt TALLER somehow, and prettier.

I remember saying things that made everyone laugh, but I don't remember what they were.

Suddenly we were all in the kitchen making more drinks.

Ryan and Blake went back to the living room and brought the coke into the kitchen. I remember doing another line with them while Lauren and Andrew made out in the corner of the kitchen.

FLASH—Running out to the hot tub with Ross. Laughing so hard I cried as he pulled off all of his clothes and jumped into the water naked with Ian.

FLASH—Another line with Lauren in the kitchen.

FLASH—Dancing with Blake on one side and Ryan on the other.

FLASH—Running into the kitchen for another line with Ross and Ian.

FLASH—Sliding down into the hot tub and realizing we're all in the hot tub. In our underwear. Nothing else.

I wasn't sure whose legs and hands were whose, but the buzz of the coke made me not really care. I felt like my face was lit up from a hum on the inside that made every word I said sound smart, and important.

Ian brought towels out and I caught myself staring at him. I'd never realized how muscular he was before. I nudged Ross and said, Your boyfriend is a hottie. He laughed and said, Let's go smoke out.

FLASH—Back in the living room, smoking a bowl. Ian sprinkling a little cocaine onto the weed in the bowl and saying, You're gonna love this. Smoking deeply, but not feeling that heavy feeling that pot always gives me.

FLASH—Making more drinks with Lauren back in the kitchen. I told her I felt like I could drink a lot more without getting really wasted. She laughed and said that was why cocaine was so awesome, but she said I should pace myself. I told her my stomach was feeling weird. She said that's because they cut the cocaine with stuff like baby laxatives so it's not 100 percent pure. She grabbed her purse and gave me another little chunk of a Xanax tablet.

FLASH—The Xanax and the pot took the edge off of the upset feeling in my stomach. I am laughing with Lauren about how drunk Andrew is, and I hug her and say, THIS IS PERFECT! She hugs me back and says, I know!

FLASH—Blake is sitting in the hot tub with me while everyone else is in the kitchen. We are staring at the lights of the city. I feel his hands on my foot under the water. He starts massaging my foot and it feels AMAZING. I lay my head back and close my eyes.

FLASH—Another bump of cocaine, this time with Ross and Blake. We're all wearing towels, and after I snort the line, I see Blake wipe the end of the straw with his finger and rub it across his top gum. He tells me to try it. The taste is metallic, like the drip in the back of my throat, but it makes my teeth numb, and suddenly I feel so clear and alive!

FLASH—Blake leaves with Lauren to go get more vodka. Ross and Ian have disappeared into the master bedroom. I'm in the hot tub with Ryan and Andrew. At first we were just laughing about the dance and Andrew is talking about school, and this house, and where he's going to college, and how he can't wait for their next volleyball tournament, and all of a sudden I feel lips on my ear and realize that Ryan has pulled me over to him, is nibbling on my ear, and it feels really good, so I lean into him and suddenly our lips have found each other and I feel his tongue on mine, and I put my arms around his neck.

As I'm kissing Ryan, I feel arms around my waist and realize that Andrew is kissing my shoulder! I try to pull away from Ryan, but he just holds me tighter, and I relax a little as I kiss him. We stay like that for a minute, and I feel the heat around my legs in the bubbling water spread up into my stomach and my chest. My breath gets shallow, and I press my mouth even harder into Ryan's. I feel Andrew moving his hands up and down on my stomach and then up to my breasts, and I pull away from Ryan and laugh. Andrew! What are you doing?

He just leans in behind me and whispers, Shhhhhhh, then smiles and says, You know you've wanted both of us since you laid eyes on us. All of a sudden my heart is pounding in my chest. I am NOT okay with this. I turn back to Ryan. I hope he will help me. I hope he will tell his friend to back the hell off. But he just winks at me and leans in to kiss me again.

I try to pull back, but Ryan tightens his grip around my waist while Andrew slides his hands down between my legs. I'm only wearing my underwear and bra, and I hear Andrew saying Sssshh as he slides his fingers under the fabric, pulling them to the side, exploring, exposing. I arch my back and try to throw him off with my hips as I push against Ryan. I yell: STOP. DON'T, ANDREW! But Ryan is pulling me down onto the seat in the hot tub. He pushes me down, hard, and I hit my back against the concrete edge of the tub.

The pain makes me go limp for a second, and Andrew takes this moment to pull my legs farther apart. Ryan is trying to kiss me again.

FLASH—Ryan's hands on my breast, kneading, pawing, squeezing.

FLASH—Andrew's breath on my neck, his fingers pushing further and further inside of me.

FLASH—Their arms holding me down. Their mouths clamped over mine, stifling my shouts. Andrew laughing as Ryan steps in between my legs, forcing them open with his. Screaming. My heart racing, where is everyone? Is Blake coming back?

FLASH—Ryan flies sideways, splashing across the hot tub. Andrew wheels around. I yell out for help. I see a fist connect with Andrew's nose. Blood spurts into the water. Cam is standing in the hot tub, fully clothed. Astrid is pulling me up onto the side of the tub, covering me with a towel.

Andrew is scrambling backward out of the tub toward his clothes. Cam has Ryan by the throat, one fist has already landed, and his arm is drawn back again. Every muscle in his body is strained. Ross and Ian are there, too, and Blake and Lauren are running toward us. Everyone arrived at once.

I've never heard Cam curse like this before: If you ever fucking look at her again . . . If you fucking look at her sideways . . . If you fucking bump into her in the hallway, your ass is MINE.

Ryan and Andrew run out. The party's over.

Cam dragged me into the kitchen. Astrid and Lauren followed us in with my clothes. I saw Cam spot the mirror covered in cocaine that was sitting on the bar in the kitchen. Everything stopped. It was like somebody threw the brakes on a semitruck going 65 miles per hour down the highway. The whole evening jackknifed across Ian's dad's kitchen, then skidded to a halt.

Cam got quiet. Really quiet. He turned to Astrid and said, I have to take my sister home right now. I'm sorry. She just looked at him and nodded. Lauren had helped me back into my clothes by this point. Cam looked at Ian and Blake and said, Who. Brought. The. Coke? One word at a time, like he might explode at any moment.

Everyone just stood there, silent. Cam grabbed my arm and said, We're out.

All the way home, he let me have it. What were you thinking? Do you know how dangerous coke is? He kept saying how he'd warned me about Ryan and Andrew, and that Lauren was a bad influence on me.

Then he said he was telling Mom and Dad.

I started sobbing, and begging. I told him that I'd do anything. He pulled the car into the driveway and turned it off, and we sat there for a minute. He told me to pull it together before we walked in just in case Mom was awake. I asked him how he was going to explain to Mom and Dad that he was wet from the waist down. He said he was going to tell them exactly what happened unless . . .

I said unless what?

He told me I had to stop. Everything. No more pot, or drinking, or pills, or anything. He said no more sneaking to Lauren's for cosmos with Astrid and Ross. They could come to our house for the next month, but that was it. If he saw anything going on, he'd tell Mom and Dad everything.

I felt desperate. I would've promised Cam ANYTHING to stay quiet. I felt my heart racing. I was so panicked that he'd tell Mom and Dad I'd done cocaine. I knew they wouldn't yell or scream. I knew they'd just look at me and tell me how disappointed they were with me. I couldn't face that. I couldn't stand to see the hurt in their eyes.

So I promised. I promised Cam that I would be done with it all.

That was late Friday night. Well, I guess it was early Saturday morning. Today is Sunday and I can't believe it's only been a day since all of this happened. From the back deck at Grams and Gramps's I can see a sailboat in the distance, a white blur against the bright blue sky. The boat seems so far away, sort of like Andrew and Ryan and what happened on Friday night.

Yesterday I just lay around with Lauren, feeling sick and sad. Somehow, today I feel numb.

Grams came out with a glass of iced tea for me. She's sitting next to me in the sun. Told me to keep writing, that it does her heart good to see how much I like it. Jeez. She'd fall over and die if she knew I was recording my first time doing cocaine and almost getting raped in a hot tub.

God. My life has become like a terrible Lifetime movie of the week.

Later . . .

We just got back from Grams and Gramps's. Lauren has been texting me all day. Ross is really worried about me. He's been hanging out with her today. Lauren wants me to come over and join them, but Cam is watching me like a hawk.

And you know something? I'm glad.

I'm glad I have a brother who was there for me on Friday night. I start crying every time I think of what would have happened if he hadn't shown up when he did.

I texted her back on the way home from Grams and Gramps's and told her that we'd regroup at lunch tomorrow with Cam. I leaned over and showed the phone to Cam before I pressed send. He read the text, then looked across the backseat and smiled at me for the first time since Friday.

Then I lay my head down on his lap and closed my eyes. I felt him put his hand on my arm and give me a little squeeze. We stayed like that for a long time, and when I opened my eyes again, we were pulling into our driveway back home.

September 26

We all made a pact today at lunch—Me, Lauren, Astrid, Ross: no more drugs. It was a fun experiment, but I'm done. It's just not worth it. Everybody agreed. Astrid said she was so glad that

Cam had shown up when he had. Lauren had tears in her eyes and said she was so sorry for even introducing me to Ryan and Andrew. Ross said that Ian and Blake felt really terrible and they are laying off the partying too.

Cam seemed satisfied, and it felt good. A clean start. It felt good to have everybody there at the table, and bonded together. I don't know what I was thinking. I guess I wanted them all to like me so much that I never considered that they'd be okay with not drinking; that they'd want to hang out with me just for the friendship part.

I have to admit it'll be strange. Most times, we've all gotten stoned together. Ross had a great idea, though—this weekend we're all going to go do yoga together on Saturday. Ian is teaching a class on Saturday morning, and Cam is jazzed about getting back into it now that soccer is winding down.

I feel happy in that satisfied, contented way that makes it seem like everything is going to be all right.

October 1

We all went to Ian's yoga class this morning. It was hard after not having been there in a while. Ian says yoga is surgery without knives, and he's right! That's what it feels like.

Afterward Cam and I went shopping for Dad's birthday

(which is today!) We got him some running shorts and a running shirt, the kind that wicks the moisture off of your skin while you sweat. Dad likes to run on the path along the beach in the mornings before he goes to teach. I'm really glad that my dad is such a health nut. It makes me feel like maybe he'll be around for a long time. I never really think about how much I like my mom and dad until I think about them not being around, and that idea is so weird that it's hard to wrap my head around it. Dad is turning 47 today. He was 30 when I was born. That seems so crazy to me.

What will I be doing when I'm 30?

I can't really imagine past being in college. I mean, I can sort of imagine myself graduating from college, but then I'm not sure what it looks like after that. I like to think about having a boyfriend.

For some reason, when I wrote that last sentence, Mark flashed into my head. Yesterday in the hall he asked me how homecoming was. I said it was fine. I asked him how it was for him. He said he went home after the soccer game.

Maybe I'll see if he wants to come to lunch with us on Monday.

Dad has invited his friend from college, Dale, and his wife, Karen, over for dinner tonight. They have a little boy named Nelson who is 9 years old. Mom is making Dad's favorite meal: lasagna, with German chocolate cake for dessert. Cam and I were allowed to invite one friend each as well. I like that about Dad. He always wants to make sure that our friends are included.

Cam invited Astrid, of course. I invited Lauren this morning after yoga class, but she said she is having dinner with her dad at some fancy place tonight, so Ross is coming instead. Mom said Lauren could come over for dessert if she gets done with her dad in time.

I texted her, but I haven't heard back. I hope she's okay. I know that the thing with Andrew and Ryan really upset her.

Later . . .

Dinner was delicious. Ross wore a bow tie, which was funny because he's got that shaggy surfer hair. He looked so cute! Mom really likes Astrid. I can tell. Astrid looked beautiful, and she always seems to know the right thing to say. She was able to talk to Karen and Dale like she had known them for years and years.

After dinner Cam and Ross took Nelson outside and kicked the soccer ball around for a while. I texted Lauren twice, but I didn't hear back from her. Weird. I'm sure she's just at dinner with her dad and some big-time rock star. Sometimes he invites her to dinner and she ends up sitting across the table from some world-famous singer.

October 3

Lauren isn't at school today. Ross and Astrid haven't heard from her either. Now I'm getting worried. I am going to walk down to her place with Ross at lunch. Mark will just have to wait.

Later . . .

The good news: Lauren is alive.

The bad news: She is not well.

When Ross and I got to her place, we signed in with the security guard at the front desk, then took the elevator up to the penthouse level. Ross banged on the door while I texted her that we were in her hallway.

Finally she came to the door. It looked like she'd been crying. Her eyes were really puffy and she was all sniffly. She said that she had gone to dinner with her dad on Saturday night and then had an allergy attack when she got home and couldn't sleep for two nights. I hugged her and told her that she should at least text me back so I don't send the Coast Guard out looking for her body.

When we were walking back to school, Ross was really quiet. I asked him if he was okay. He nodded and said he was fine, but he thought that Lauren wasn't.

I asked him what he meant, and he said it didn't look like an allergy attack to him. He said he thought it looked like Lauren had been partying. And by partying he meant cocaine.

I told him that was ridiculous. We'd all just made that pact last week.

Ross just shook his head and smiled at me, this weird smile like he thought what I said was sweet but that I just didn't get it. I told him he was crazy. He told me I hadn't been around cocaine very much. I asked him when he'd become such an expert, but right at that moment Mark walked up with Cam and Astrid. I told them that Lauren was fine; she'd just had an allergy attack. Ross snorted and rolled his eyes. Cam saw him and frowned, then asked what was up. Ross just shook his head and said, Nothing. A little Benadryl will fix her right up. Then he walked off to class.

GOD. Ross can be such a DICK sometimes.

October 7

School SUCKED this week. God. I am so happy I don't have to go back tomorrow, but I have so much homework, I won't be able to leave the house this weekend.

Lauren was back in class on Tuesday looking stunning as usual. Ross was sorta standoffish and quiet all week. He kept watching Lauren when she talked, like he was looking for clues. Astrid and Cam are spending a lot of time together, which is nice. I really like her. She's coming over later to watch a movie with Cam, which is code for lie on the couch under a blanket and do God knows what. I have to write two papers this weekend—one for history and one for English. I don't have any idea how I'm going to get them done.

When I told Mom about it, she was very sweet and said she'd take me out to sushi on Sunday night to celebrate finishing.

I told her the thing that might be finished by then is ME.

I always feel so good when I make my mom laugh.

October 9

It's 4 p.m. and I feel like my fingers are going to fall off from typing school papers. And that my brain is going to leak out of my ears. It actually feels good to hold this pen and write on paper that isn't virtual. I have to finish the bibliography for the English paper and then I am DONE.

Later . . .

Just got back from sushi with Mom. In the middle of dinner she started asking more questions about homecoming. She said I had seemed sort of quiet after that night and wanted to know how my date with Ryan went. When she said his name, my heart started racing like I had been running a marathon and I felt all sick to my stomach. She asked me if I was feeling okay, and I said I was fine, but I wasn't. Just the thought of him pushing me down in that hot tub gives me a panic attack.

I told her that Ryan just wasn't my type. We're not a match.

Now I'm freaking out. I'm not sure how I'm going to get to sleep thinking about that all night. Jesus. I'd just started to forget it. I wish my parents didn't want to do such a Good Job parenting sometimes. I mean, I know you're supposed to ask your kids questions and stay engaged in their lives, but some things I just don't want to talk about.

I wish Ross were here right now with his pipe so we could smoke a bowl. I know I promised Cam that I wouldn't smoke out anymore, but UGH. This SUCKS.

Later . . .

It's 1 a.m. and I'm still not asleep. I'm going to be a zombie at school tomorrow.

Later . . .

1:30 a.m.

I just texted Lauren to see if she's still awake. No response.

Then I texted Blake 'cause he used to send me texts in the middle of the night all the time. I guess he's always up late playing music with his band and stuff?

He texted right back. I haven't really heard from him since

the Homecoming Hot Tub Fiasco. He asked what I was doing up. I said I couldn't sleep. He wrote back:

SLEEPING IS OVERRATED . . . ;)

October 10

Elizabeth Archer just poked me in the back with her finger because I was asleep in class. Ross is sitting in front of me and I had laid my head down on my desk. How do teachers expect you to stay awake when they turn off the lights and close the blinds so that they can use a projector? Thank God I have this journal to write in so I can stay awake.

Mark walked me to class this morning. He was hanging out by our lockers when Lauren and I walked in today. Lauren saw him standing there and elbowed me. She said, Don't look now, but All-American Mark is lying in wait. Then she giggled. She's taken to calling him All-American Mark, and he does look like something out of an Abercrombie ad. At least he doesn't use their cologne. I can always smell that crap a mile down the hallway. The boys in my school are obsessed with it—that and Axe body spray. Ross has a theory that they wear it because they think it will make them look like the guys in the commercials for it. The guys in the ads all have chiseled muscles and look like they haven't ever eaten a french fry in their lives. Cam looks like that, mainly because he runs nonstop and plays soccer. Thankfully he doesn't wear too much of anything that smells too strong.

Anyway, when Lauren and I walked up, I invited Mark to come to lunch. He frowned and said, Isn't the guy supposed to ask the girl out?

Lauren snort-laughed when he said this. I just looked at him until he said, What?

Lauren said, Oh nothing. Maybe after lunch you can slay a dragon for us and kill the evil witch. What century are you living in?

Which was funny, but it made Mark blush, and for some reason I feel badly about that. I'm not sure why. I mean, he's SOOOO old-fashioned in some ways, but there's something about it that seems . . . I dunno. Sweet? Yeah, it seems sweet, like he wants to be Proper with a capital P.

I'm just not sure what he sees in a girl like me. It makes me wonder why he's so interested.

October 16

I can't believe I haven't written in almost a week.

Actually, yes I can. Midterms start tomorrow.

I'm doomed.

October 19

YAAAAAAAAAY!

MIDTERMS ARE OVER!

Ross and Lauren and I are going to the movies tonight.
Astrid and Cam might join us. I am SO RELIEVED. I don't
think I did very well on chemistry. We had a marathon study
session at our place last night. Astrid, Lauren, and I all sat at
the dining room table until Lauren actually fell asleep with her
head on a book and I couldn't see the flash cards Astrid was
holding to drill us. (Astrid is crazy when it comes to studying.
Who makes flash cards?)

We blew up the air mattress in my room for Astrid,
and Lauren slept in my bed with me. I got up to go to the
bathroom in the middle of the night, and no one was on the
air mattress. This morning in the kitchen, Mom was making
us a big "Last Day of Midterms" breakfast (BEST. MOM.
EVER.) and I pulled Cam aside and said, So . . . funny thing.
Astrid wasn't on the air mattress when I got up to go to the
bathroom last night. He didn't even LOOK at me, just poured
some coffee and said, I have no idea what you're talking about,
little sister.

But his ears were bright red.

LOL. Gotcha.

Later . . .

Ian showed up at the movie last night. Ross doesn't talk a lot about what's going on with the two of them, and he hadn't really mentioned Ian since homecoming. It was a little tense because Cam showed up too, and he's still a little touchy about Ian and the whole cocaine thing. But we went to the movie, and then out to get milk shakes and french fries at Swingers. Mom let us stay out until midnight, even though it was a school night. By the time we were all piled into the booth at the restaurant, Cam and Ian were joking around again and things seemed back to normal.

Then Ian dropped the bomb: Blake is throwing a giant Halloween party.

Lauren threw both hands up in the air and squealed like an 8-year-old.

Cam got really quiet. Lauren saw this and said, Oh, don't worry, Cam. We all took the pact, remember? No scary party drugs. Besides! You and Astrid will be there.

Cam shook his head and looked uneasy.

Astrid put her arm around him and buried her nose in his neck.

Whatever she whispered to him were the magic words, 'cause his ears went red again and he got this sort of wicked-looking smirk on his face.

I smiled at him across the table and said, I promise we'll be good, Cam. I PROMISE.

He grinned at me, but there was caution in his eyes. He said he wasn't worried about me being good. It was the rest of these yahoos he had to keep an eye on.

OMG! I'M SO EXCITED. This Halloween party is going to ROCK.

Let the costume planning commence!

October 22

I think my feet might fall off. We walked up and down to every costume store on Hollywood Blvd. today to get the stuff for our costumes, but it was SO WORTH IT.

We're going to Halloween as a HAUNTED CIRCUS.

Lauren: Ring Mistress Dominatrix

Ross: Lion

Me: Sexy Clown

Astrid and Cam are going as Antony and Cleopatra. Jason and Elizabeth Archer are coming too, but I'm not sure what their costumes are going to be yet.

Cam is really excited about the party now. I think he just needed some reassurance from me that we're all staying on the straight edge. Well . . . mainly.

I wasn't even sure if I should write this down, but after we got our costumes, Lauren and Ross and I were in his truck on the way back. (Cam and Astrid went in Cam's car.) Anyway, Ross had his pipe and smoked us out.

I don't think Cam would really care, but I'd rather not give him any reason to be upset, so that'll just be our little secret.

God! I forgot how great it is to get stoned and laugh my ass off with Lauren and Ross.

Cannot. Wait. For. Next. Weekend!

November 1

I feel so fucked up right now, like I don't know what's right and what's wrong anymore. Thank God Cam left early last night. I'm still in deep shit with him as it is, but at least he doesn't know about the Ecstasy yet, and if I can help it he WON'T.

Lauren did a really good job talking Cam down over the last week. He was still a little leery of going to Blake's for the Halloween party because of the whole homecoming thing, but most every day at lunch last week Lauren and Astrid talked about their costumes, and how great the music was going to be, and blah blah blah. Cam was finally getting really excited.

Everybody came over here to get ready last night before we went to Blake's. Mom and Dad could not take enough pictures. Lauren looked AMAZING in her black shiny vinyl high-heeled boots that went up to her thighs, and her fishnets. She wore a black leotard with a bow tie and a tuxedo jacket that had long tails. Her top hat was bright red, and she had this long gold whip that was wound up and hung from her belt. She piled her long blond hair up on top of her head in a tight French twist with little ringlets down the side of her face and crazy dramatic eye makeup. She was a KNOCKOUT.

I could tell Mom thought Lauren's costume was a little trampy because when we were planning what I would wear, she made sure that mine covered a little bit more skin, which was fine with me. My body's nowhere near as amazing as Lauren's is, but my costume was so FUN! I had a tiny purple skirt that poofed out with crinolines underneath. I wore bright red fishnets and heels that Lauren loaned me. The shoes were this vintage pair of old-fashioned character heels that made my legs look great! I had a silver corset and loooooooong fake eyelashes. Astrid and Lauren spent like an hour curling my hair into these tiny ringlets that they pinned up in the back so they could perch a tiny clown hat with a GIANT plume sticking out of the top. I had white face paint and tiny red heart lips, sort of like a clown from Paris. At least that was the idea according to Ross who found this picture online. I also had a tiny parasol. When we were all done, I looked in the mirror and hardly recognized myself. I looked amazing.

I realized while I was getting ready that my tummy was all

jumpy, and every time I looked in the mirror, I realized I was thinking about what Blake would think when he looked at me. I kept remembering our kiss by the hot tub on homecoming night. He had pulled me in so tight, and kissed me so hard, like he was drowning and I was the only way he could get oxygen. He texted me yesterday and said, CAN'T WAIT 2 C U.

I was texting him back when Ross came out of the bathroom where Astrid and Lauren were doing his makeup. Ross had a fake fur mane and was covered in gold glittery powder dusted on his face and bare chest. He had skin-tight black jeans that had a tail sewn onto the back that Lauren linked to his wrist with a little bit of clear fishing line that Astrid got out of her dad's tackle box. (Astrid and Lauren are like crafting GENIUSES.)

Astrid had this AWESOME black Cleopatra wig that had straight bangs. Her long linen robe had a jeweled collar. She looked like some sort of Egyptian goddess. Lauren had found these gold snakes with wires in them that we wrapped around her arms and wrists.

When Cam came out in his Mark Antony Roman war-hero getup, Lauren and Astrid and Mom and I hooted and whistled. He was wearing sandals that had long leather straps that wrapped all the way up to his knees and a short tunic with armor that covered his chest. The breastplate was shiny plastic, but it looked like metal and he had a shield and a helmet with red plumage at the top.

Mom and Dad took pictures like somebody was getting married; then they made everyone promise to drive the speed limit.

Cam and Astrid drove to Blake's together, and Lauren drove me and Ross. When we got to Blake's and parked, I still couldn't believe the view. My stomach was all jumpy because I hadn't seen Blake in a long time, but BOOM: There he was. He was dressed as a mummy . . . or I guess I should say UNdressed as a mummy because very little of him was actually covered. He had these strategically placed strips of cloth wrapped around his head, arms, and legs, but his chest was mainly bare. I just stared. I guess I had been pretty drunk and high the last time I was here and we were in his bathroom together. I hadn't really noticed what an AMAZING body he has.

Then, my stomach REALLY got jumpy because Cam walked right up to him and I realized I was holding my breath until they smiled at each other and shook hands. Then Blake winked at me and threw his arm around Cam's shoulders and showed him around. The tour was equally impressive the second time around, only this time there were WILD Halloween decorations everywhere. There were black lights making stuff glow purple and the pool lights had red gels in them so the water looked like blood as it flowed off the false edge of the concrete deck. But even cooler than the pool was something that Blake had kept a surprise:

There was a giant bouncy castle inflated next to the pool. There were already 3 or 4 people in it jumping up and down and screaming like maniacs. Lauren and Astrid and I were like NO WAY. Cam just shook his head and gave Blake a high five. Ross didn't even wait. He'd seen that Ian was one of the guys in the castle and took off running in a cloud of gold body glitter.

Astrid and Cam were talking to Blake, and Lauren and I wandered down to the clear glass wall at the end of the pool. The moon was a tiny waning crescent (SEE? I DID learn something last year in physical science), and there was an eerie blanket of fog rolling in off the ocean. It was PERFECT for a Halloween party.

I leaned close to her, and our arms touched. I said, Remember? This is where we met. She threw her head back and laughed, and hugged me. She said, I can't even remember not knowing you. What did I do for fun before you?

Couldn't focus on the fog for very long because right about that moment, the DJ started spinning. YES. There was a DJ. One of Blake's friends (who also has a deal with Lauren's dad's record label) was spinning. Lauren and I stood there looking around as people in the CRAZIEST costumes poured out onto the dance floor that was set up near the house. Lauren grabbed my hand and yelled cosmos!, then we took off running for the kitchen.

Cam and Astrid were already there with Blake. The guys had beers and looked like best friends. Astrid was drinking sparkling water, and when Lauren offered her a cosmo, she just shook her head and winked, then whispered, I'm going to try to get Mark Antony out of here a little early to have some ALONE time. Lauren said that she'd drink to that, and we clinked glasses, then pushed everybody out onto the dance floor and danced our asses off.

Ross and Ian joined us and Ian had gold body glitter all over his costume because he'd been jumping around in the bouncy castle with Ross. Ross pulled Cam aside and the two of them disappeared for a little while, and I KNEW that they were smoking out.

I got SO JEALOUS at that second. I mean, how can CAM be telling ME not to do drugs and smoke out and hang with these guys if he's going to do it? I tapped Lauren on the shoulder and said, Did you see Cam and Ross just leave to go smoke out? She smiled a wicked Ring Mistress smile, then adjusted her top hat with one hand as she pressed a little chunk of Xanax into my palm with the other hand and said, One step ahead of you, sister.

I looked down at the tiny pill in my hand. I said, What about our PACT? She said, We've been really good! We've proven that we can handle it. Besides, it's not like we're doing coke or something.

I felt weird about it, like I wasn't sure what would happen if I took this little pill, but the music was so loud, and we looked so good, and Lauren was laughing and dancing and telling me to C'MON!

I grinned at her and we danced over to Astrid who was refilling her sparkling water in the kitchen. Lauren scooted around a man dressed as a rapping rhinoceros and grabbed the martini shaker. She mixed us an extra-strong round of cosmos and we washed down our Xanax. Ross came around the corner with Cam. I raised an eyebrow and asked, How is the smoke this evening?

Cam was totally caught and he knew it. He looked at Ross, then back at me and said, Okay, but just a couple tokes. I don't want you throwing up again.

I raised my cosmo glass and said, No, no. It's fine. I don't need to smoke pot to be cool.

Lauren and Astrid cracked up. Cam just rolled his eyes and shook his head, then Astrid led him back out to the dance floor.

Ross asked if I wanted to get stoned, but I didn't. I realized that I was just jealous that Ross had asked Cam first, and I was pissed that Cam was trying to act like my dad or something by telling me that I should stay totally clean while he went and had fun. I told Ross that maybe I'd want to later. I remembered how NOT fun it was to throw up on the way home. My clown outfit was way too cute for that. Ross pulled me into the living room where we started dancing with two girls who were dressed as sexy cats.

Blake, Ian, and Lauren came over, then Cam and Astrid joined us. We all danced our way out by the pool, and slowly everyone in our party became covered in Ross the Lion's gold body glitter. At some point I had put down my parasol in the kitchen, and Lauren's top hat wound up on Blake's head. Blake kept dancing back and forth to the kitchen with a shaker of cosmos, and Lauren kept making sure our glasses were full. Cam must've been on his 4th beer when Astrid checked her phone and whispered in Cam's ear.

I don't know what she said, but it worked. He came dancing over to talk to me. Actually, he walked like an Egyptian over to me, following Astrid, who held his hand over her shoulder. His breath was hot on my cheek and smelled like beer, but his smile was so wide, I couldn't resist smiling back. Astrid was going to drive him back to Egypt, he said, giggling. Then he tried to get as stern as he could after 4 beers and made sure that Ian knew how important it was that I got home by 1 a.m. because that was curfew and he'd promised Mom and Dad that he'd look out for me. He turned to leave with Astrid and then pulled Ian in close and yelled over the music: Don't make me regret this.

Lauren ran up and hugged Astrid, then kissed Cam on the nose and said she'd take good care of me. Cam rolled his eyes and said that's what he was afraid of. Then Lauren dragged me down to the bouncy castle, and before I knew it, we'd kicked off our high heels and we were jumping around, shrieking and laughing like idiots. It made me think of when I was a little girl at the carnival down by the pier at the beach. Cam had eaten too many hot dogs and got a stomachache from jumping around too fast, but Dad had to come in and drag me out when it was time to go home. I never wanted to leave.

Lauren double-bounced me at one point, and I crashed into her, then we both collapsed and lay on our backs laughing and listening to the music. She propped up on her elbow and asked me if I thought Astrid and Cam were going to go all the way tonight. I was like, AAAUGH. He's my BROTHER! And she giggled and tickled me between my corset and my skirt until I yelled that I was going to wet my pants if she didn't stop. She grabbed my hand and said, Why didn't you TELL me you had to go to the bathroom. C'MON!

We went running into the house. Blake called to us, but Lauren was on a mission. We ran up the stairs to Blake's bedroom and closed the door. I was peeing while Lauren reapplied her lipstick, and when I stepped over to the sink, she opened the cabinet under the vanity and pulled out a mirror that had a giant pile of white powder on it. She shot me a mischievous smile and asked if I wanted a bump.

I stopped short and asked, Where'd that come from? She said Blake told her he always has a stash under the sink at parties.

I could hear the music down by the pool, but it sounded so far away, like the DJ was on the moon. I watched as Lauren used the razor blade Blake had left behind to cut lines, bigger than the ones we had done the night of homecoming. Then she picked up a little glass tube that was lying on the mirror and snorted one of the lines—half of it up each nostril. She did a little head shake that made her ringlets bounce, then turned and motioned me over.

I felt my throat get tight. It was CRAZY. I wanted to snort that line SO BADLY, but I stood there frozen. I told her I couldn't. She laughed, and said, Of COURSE you can. Cam's gone. Nobody will know. And it'll make you feel DELICIOUS.

The thing was that I knew she was right. I remembered after homecoming how I'd felt like a rock star when I had my first line. I felt like I was a giant magnet and I could pull anybody to me that I wanted. Every word I said sounded hilarious, and smart, and made people love me.

And then I remembered the hot tub: Andrew's hands on my butt, the hard edge of the hot tub digging into my back as Ryan tried to force my legs apart, and I felt like I was going to throw up. Lauren saw the look on my face and put the coke back under the sink, then ran over and hugged me. She whispered into my ear, said that it was okay. That she was so sorry that happened. That I didn't have to do anything I didn't want to.

As we stood there, I felt her arms around me and I felt better. I started to breathe a little slower, and the memory of the terrible drip from the coke in my throat on homecoming night finally subsided.

There was a knock on the bathroom door, and we heard Blake's voice asking if everybody was okay. Lauren pulled back and asked if I was okay. I nodded and smiled. She opened the door, and Ross and Ian and Blake pushed into the bathroom and closed the door again. Ross had his pipe and a Baggie of weed out before I could say hello, and I realized that was exactly what I wanted. Ross packed a bowl, and I took a long deep hit, and then another. Instantly I felt more calm.

Blake had brought up the martini shaker and a couple of glasses. The vodka was so cold against my lips after the smoke, and it tasted like SweeTarts. I had a big gulp, and felt the icy splash on my tongue. Lauren's eyes were wide, and darting around. I knew she was feeling the buzz from the coke. My eyes felt a little droopy, but I wasn't sleepy, I was relaxed. I sat down on the edge of the bathtub as Ian and Ross repacked the bowl of weed, and I felt warm strong hands on my bare shoulders. It was Blake.

His hands felt so good massaging my neck and shoulders. I closed my eyes and leaned back against him. He was standing in the tub and I felt his lips on my neck, then his breath against my ear: You look so beautiful.

When I opened my eyes, Ross was smoking the pipe, and Ian was offering Lauren a mint from a little red tin he'd opened up. She popped one in her mouth and sucked on it, then her eyes got wide and she swigged the last of her cosmo. One gulp and the mint was gone.

Ian was laughing, and Lauren playfully smacked his arm. I asked what was wrong with the mint. She said, Nothing, it just wasn't a mint. Genius here just gave me a tab of E.

Maybe it was the pot, or Blake's hands working the tension out of my neck, but I guess I didn't understand right away what she meant. Then it hit me: Ecstasy.

I sat up on the edge of the tub and looked around. Ian was still laughing, and Ross was sitting down with his back against the cabinets in the bathroom, holding the pot pipe in one hand and watching his other hand as it ran back and forth across Blake's plush silver bath mat.

I looked at Lauren and said, They're all on Ecstasy, aren't they?

Lauren followed my gaze to Ross, then Ian, and then she looked at Blake and sighed, nodding. She said that it looked like everybody was rolling but me.

I knew right away that I was not going to just sit there while everybody else did Ecstasy—no matter what I had promised Cam. I stood up from the side of the tub and held out my hand to Ian, who looked at me, then down at my hand, and then smiled when he understood.

Without a word, he pulled the red tin out of his pocket and opened it.

The pills really did look a lot like mints. It was a smart way to carry them around. He plucked one out of the pile. It had a little heart stamped into it. He smiled as he dropped it into my hand and said, Enjoy the ride.

Lauren grabbed my arm as I lifted the pill toward my lips. She asked if I was sure. In response, I put the tablet on my tongue and took a long drink of my cosmo. She jumped up and squealed, THIS is why I LOVE you.

We all went back downstairs to dance, and after about 20 or 30 minutes, I was feeling hot, and a little drunk, but nothing else. I went to the kitchen and grabbed a bottle of water out of Blake's fridge. The clock on the microwave was glowing a bright blue 11:47, and I realized at that there was no way that I was going to get home at the right time tonight.

The party had thinned out a little, and I found Lauren by the pool and pulled her into the kitchen. I told her I needed a favor. She just smiled and shook her head and said not to worry. The minute I'd swallowed that tab of E she knew we weren't going home before 4 a.m., and she'd called Cam to tell him that I was spending the night at her place.

YES! I threw my arms over my head and spun around in a circle, and it felt like a big wave of pure happy crashed down on top of me. I almost felt like I was going to cry because I was so happy. When I looked up, Ross, Ian, and Blake were standing behind Lauren in the kitchen watching me spin around. I caught myself, and said, WHAT?

Ross handed me a grape-flavored candy lollipop and said, Feeling anything yet?

I took the sucker and unwrapped it and put it in my mouth as I thought about it and said, I don't know. But Ross! This sucker tastes AMAZING!

They all burst out laughing, and Blake said, You're rolling!

And it was like the minute he said that I felt another big wave of pure happiness crash over me, stronger this time. It made my knees feel weak and my jaw a little clenched—almost like I was going over the first drop on a roller coaster, and I was glad that I had the sucker in my mouth. This wave made me take a great big deep breath, and suddenly I felt a wave of heat that made my forehead a little sweaty and I took another big deep breath. The waves were coming with my breath and Lauren took my hand and said, C'mon! Let's go outside.

As I stepped out onto the back stairs that went down to the pool, a crisp breeze came blowing off of the water and the red lights of the pool seemed to glow brighter in a flash. The grape sucker in my mouth tasted like the best thing I'd ever put on my tongue, and Lauren's hand felt so soft in my mine. Suddenly I stopped and closed my eyes and took another deep breath as a big wave of intense feeling rolled through my body.

I felt Blake's hands on my shoulder, and my eyes flew open. The lights in the pool flashed 100 times brighter than they had been, and as I looked up at the sliver of moon reflecting off of the ocean, my eyes wiggled back and forth really quickly for just a second, and I saw these AMAZING streamers of light flying off the moon and the lights in the pool. I felt Blake's lips at my ear, and my whole body shivered like I was cold, but I wasn't.

Blake whispered, This is why they call it Ecstasy.

And as he said it, I felt another wave of pure happiness wash over me, and I realized THIS is why they say you're ROLLING. I pulled Lauren's hand closer to me and said, It's coming in WAVES!

I've always had fun dancing, but after a couple of songs, I get bored, or sweaty, or tired, and usually take a break. Dancing on E was like NOTHING I'd ever experienced. I couldn't get my body close enough to Blake's or to Lauren's. Every touch felt like an electric wave of tiny tingles that spread slowly up my fingers and arms down my whole body into my legs and feet. The music sounded like something coming from inside of me. I wasn't HEARING the music, I was FEELING the music, and we danced, and danced, and danced, until all our makeup had sweated off, and we'd kicked off our shoes, and Blake had wrapped his arms around me. I felt like I could dance all night long.

The funny thing is that writing this now, there are so many problems that I can think of. There are so many things that I feel aren't right about me, about my life, about how I look, about how I feel, about my friends, about my family. I have so many fears, and worries, and I think too much about all of those things.

But dancing by the pool with Blake and Lauren, and Ross and Ian, I didn't worry. At all. I wasn't afraid. Of anything. It wasn't that I had all the answers to all of my questions, it was that I didn't have any questions. Everything felt like it made sense, and not just in my head, it made sense in my heart, in a way that I can't explain. My stomach was calm and I felt a beautiful, glorious, peaceful excitement. Peaceful excitement? I sound like a CRAZY person. But that's what it was like—that there was nothing wrong. It felt like "wrong" wasn't even an option, as if nothing had ever been wrong, or ever COULD be wrong.

At some point, we all ended up in the jumping castle. If bouncing around had been fun BEFORE, it was AMAZING on Ecstasy. As I jumped up and down, the lights at the pool squiggled in bright plumes around me. My eyes would wiggle back and forth really fast a couple times a minute, and great big waves of happiness swept over me until I was breathless.

Finally we all collapsed in a heap in the castle and lay there talking, talking, talking. Ross talked about how glad he was that he'd met Ian, and Ian talked about how he couldn't believe that Ross was into him, and when I looked up, he had the most beautiful smile and there were tears sliding down his cheeks. His whole face looked lit up from the inside, and his eyes almost seemed to be glowing.

I felt so happy in that moment that Ross and Ian had found each other. Lauren took my hand, and Blake pressed his body against mine on the other side and ran a hand through my hair. I said how great it was that I'd met Lauren and Ross this summer, and suddenly my eyes were filled with the happiest, warmest tears I'd ever felt. I had to take several deep breaths as I talked. Lauren had tears in her eyes too. As the drops brimmed over my eyelids and slid down my cheeks, they felt thick and warm, like syrup or glycerin, and another wave of pure joy washed over me. We all lay there for a few minutes listening to the music, and then Blake said:

Let's go put our feet in the hot tub.

So we did.

The DJ was playing slower songs now, and people were leaving.

Somebody gave me a water bottle, and the warmth of the hot tub on my feet and legs felt like a delicious caress. Lauren and I talked and talked about how wonderful it felt, and how amazing this night was, and how we wished that Astrid and Cam were here with us. Slowly, somehow, it got quiet. The music finally faded away, and everyone left, and Lauren looked at me and smiled. She didn't even have to say any words. It was just the two of us sitting here under the moon. And I felt so connected to her, like we'd be best friends forever.

Blake must've seen everyone out and paid the DJ, because he came to the back door and said, Hey you guys! C'mere.

Lauren and I got up and walked into the house, and there in the living room, Ross and Ian were lying on the shiny silver shag rug in the living room. The fibers were thin and stringy, soft and smooth. I don't really remember how it happened, but soon we were all lying on the rug. It felt SO GOOD running our hands and feet through it.

We stayed there for a long time on the rug. Blake disappeared into the kitchen and brought back ice cold cosmos for me and Lauren. I remember drinking it and thinking that my eyes hadn't gone wiggly in a little while. And then Blake was back on the rug with me, running his hands over the long silky silver fibers, and over my skin. Then we were kissing, and I closed my eyes and felt his body pressed against mine, and it was like we were moving together and breathing together and thinking together. His tongue felt so amazing against my own, and his hands were electric on my body.

I felt his fingers unlacing the corset of my costume, and I looked around and realized that everyone else was out back in the hot tub, and it was just us. Then we're upstairs somehow in Blake's bedroom, and sinking, sinking, sinking down into the soft mattress. I'm naked, and Blake is naked, and he's pressed against me so tight that it makes me gasp. His breath is on my ear and neck, and his hands are on my breasts. My arms are wrapped around him, my fingers sliding down his back and across his thighs, pulling him into me closer and closer until I feel like we have somehow merged into one another. I can't feel where I start and he stops, and the waves of warmth and feeling roll through me and I have never felt like this before, but I never want it to stop, and then . . .

I wake up.

When I opened my eyes, the light was bright outside the window. I lay there for a minute before I remembered where I was. I had a terrible headache and my jaw felt sore, like I had been gritting my teeth all night. I felt so achy and I stretched my legs slowly under the covers. I felt an arm around my waist and suddenly I realized that I was in Blake's bed. With Blake.

He ran his hand up and down my back, and whispered how beautiful my body is, and how amazing I felt last night, and in a flash I remembered:

We had sex.

I froze, and my stomach dropped, but not in a happy way. My head hurt so badly that I closed my eyes for a minute. Blake gave me a soft kiss on the forehead and slipped out of bed into the bathroom. I heard the shower turn on, and I grabbed my underwear off of the floor. It was the only thing I saw of mine in the room. Then I remembered the rug.

I pulled a blanket off of the bed and wrapped it around my shoulders and headed downstairs. My phone and purse were on the counter in the kitchen. I walked into the living room and felt a flood of relief when I saw Lauren curled up on the couch under a blanket.

Then I was shaking her awake, and we both checked our phones and it was after noon. The only thing that went running through my head was that I needed to find my skirt and shoes.

I collected the pieces of my costume, pulled the skirt on, and carried the corset back upstairs.

Blake came out of the bathroom in a towel as I sat down on the edge of the bed to buckle my shoes. He asked why I was leaving so soon. I asked if he had a T-shirt I could borrow so I didn't have to lace myself back into the corset, and as he fished through a dresser drawer, I realized there was something else in my head besides the pounding:

A nagging question.

As it formed in my brain, it sank down into my stomach, and I felt another wave wash over me. This one was a wave of pure undiluted terror that forced the words from my stomach up into my mouth and flying out of my lips:

Blake? Did we use a condom?

The way he smiled at me was different from the smiles I'd seen from him before. He handed me the T-shirt, and he tried to lean in and kiss my neck. I pushed away from him and looked into his eyes.

He said, What? You're on the pill, right?

The room started to spin a little bit when he said it, and I took a step backward. My cheeks were hot and I gulped a deep breath. Blake saw the answer before I even said the word no.

He shook his head and snorted a short laugh through his nose. He looked at me like I was the silliest, stupidest girl he'd ever met.

As Lauren drove us down the highway along the coast, I couldn't help but think that he was right. Lauren grabbed my hand and held it as I told her everything. She told me that I didn't need to worry: She had morning-after pills at home. She got them from her doctor in New York.

I leaned my head against the window and just stared at the gray clouds and the angry waves that pummeled the rocks along the beach where I first went to watch Ross surf. I thought about that girl who'd sat on the sand and watched Ross ride that day. She was so different from this girl: the one who had done Ecstasy last night, and had sex with a 20-year-old with no condom. This girl who was going to her best friend's house to take a morning-after pill.

Who am I now?

How did this happen?

That's when Cam texted me: WHERE ARE YOU?

I texted back: AT LAUREN'S.

He called me, and when I answered, he yelled into the phone: NO YOU'RE NOT!

When I didn't answer his texts this morning, he'd driven over to Lauren's and knocked on the door. Her dad told him that Lauren had spent the night at a friend's last night and that I wasn't there.

I hung up on him. We raced back to Lauren's, I gulped

down the morning-after pill, then she dropped me off at home.

Mom and Dad met me at the door, and I was terrified that Cam had already told them I hadn't actually spent the night at Lauren's, but he hadn't. They wanted to hear all about the party. The very last thing on the entire earth that I wanted to do was sit down to brunch with Mom and Dad and tell them about the party, but as I did, I realized they didn't know that Cam had left early with Astrid.

By the time we were done eating, I felt terrible. My headache had gotten steadily worse after I took the pill, and now I felt sick to my stomach. I was dizzy as I left the table, but Cam followed me to my room and hissed: What the HELL are you thinking? Did you spend the night at Blake's?

I just stared at him and then said, Why do you care?

His face got bright red and he said, I swear to God, if I find out that asshole laid one finger on you, I'll kill him.

I told him to calm down. That I could take care of myself.

He left in a huff, and I've been lying here, thinking about last night, and trying not to throw up.

Blake just texted me. He says he wants to see me again soon. Tonight. I texted him back and told him I have homework to do. We have essays due in American government tomorrow. It's the last thing I want to do.

All I want right now is to feel Blake's arms around me

again. I want to hear him tell me I'm beautiful. I want to feel those amazing waves of pure happiness crash over me again and again.

I don't care what Cam says.

I don't care what anybody says.

November 2

Didn't finish my American government essay. I've never not turned in an essay before. Lauren didn't have hers either. Mr. Daniels made us stay after class so he could talk to us. He told us we could hand it in during class on Thursday or he'd drop our scores one letter grade.

I don't care about Abraham Lincoln and the treaty that ended the Civil War. Writing this essay is going to be like pulling teeth.

Blake keeps texting me.

I haven't texted him back. Lauren says I should play it cool. I really want to see him again, but I am still pissed at him for not using a condom.

November 3

I handed in my freaking essay this morning.

While I was proofreading it last night after dinner, Blake

texted me. He was driving through our neighborhood. I decided that I deserved a little reward for finishing my essay, so I met him down at the end of the block, got in his car, and made out with him for a minute. He had a one-hitter with him, a little metal tube that was painted to look like a cigarette. He loaded it a few times, and we smoked out and talked and kissed for a while. I was maybe gone for like fifteen minutes. No big whoop. If Mom saw me come back inside, I was gonna tell her I was looking for my gym bag in her car.

When I walked through the door, Cam was standing in the entryway with his arms crossed. He came to my bedroom and gave me the 3rd degree. Said he followed me out and saw me get in Blake's car. Asked what was going on with me. Threatened to tell Mom and Dad that I was going out with a 20-year-old.

I told him he was being a moron and that if he said a single word to Mom and Dad I would make sure that they knew he and Astrid had left the Halloween party without me and that he was wasted so Astrid had to drive.

Thank God Cam's got his big invitational soccer tournament out of town this weekend. That means he'll leave tomorrow with the team after school and be gone until late on Sunday night. I need a break from him.

November 4

This.

Day.

Will.

Never.

END.

Lauren and I have one more class after this one: choir. Then we're going to her place with Ross, and Blake and Ian are going to meet us there. Lauren's dad is in New York for the weekend, and Astrid is going to watch Cam play soccer, so it's going to just be us.

This week I have felt like I'm walking around under Jell-O. I just want to feel good again. At lunch I asked Ross if he had pot to bring to Lauren's tonight. He smirked and said, But what about the pact?

Lauren rolled her eyes and laughed, but something about his question stuck in my stomach. I realized I wanted to feel good, and it didn't matter how much I promised myself I didn't want to do drugs anymore. What did it matter? What was the point of being so good? Wasn't it so I wouldn't do stupid things like sleep with boys with no condom? And I'd taken care of that. I can handle this. I can make my own decisions. I don't need Cam or anybody else telling me what to do. If I want to have a drink or do a line, or smoke a joint, it's nobody else's business but mine.

I must've made a funny face because Ross asked me if I was okay, said he was just teasing. I said the pact was pretty much broken last weekend.

I cannot wait for this class to be over. All I have left today is choir with Lauren, then we're headed to her place. First stop: cosmos. And some weed. Then I'm gonna drag Blake into the master bedroom and make out with him. Maybe more.

Lauren asked me how the sex was the other day. I told her that I thought it was incredible, but of course I don't have anything to compare it to. She said that if it was good, it was good, and that I shouldn't question it. She said you don't have to have lots of experience to know when something feels right.

I always feel like she has way more experience than I do. She's like this grown-up version of a teenager. She never makes me feel like a moron, though. She's always really kind to me. In all of this craziness, she's been the one person I can count on.

Lauren's friendship makes me feel really special, like I'm worth it.

November 5

~~I am so upset I don't even know how to put it into writing. I can't even sit up and hold my pen. I can't stop cry.~~

LAUREN IS A FUCKING BITCH.

179

November 6

I am never speaking to Lauren again.

I am never speaking to Blake again.

I am never doing drugs again.

Cam had a gut feeling about Lauren and Blake and Ian, and he was RIGHT about ALL of them. I feel so shitty for not believing him. I should have listened. I should have trusted him. Instead, I trusted these so-called FRIENDS.

I'm not even making any sense. If anyone ever read this (which would be like my WORST NIGHTMARE) they would think I am a lunatic. Maybe I am a lunatic. Maybe I'm the stupidest woman to have ever drawn a breath on the planet.

I don't even want to write about it.

I don't want to think about it.

I don't want to feel this feeling in my stomach. I can't eat. I can't sleep. I can't think.

Mom thinks I have the flu. She keeps coming to my room with saltines and 7Up and asking if I want any soup. She's being SO SWEET to me, and it just makes me feel EVEN WORSE for doing all of these things that she would be so upset about.

I can't stop crying.

I HATE THIS FEELING.

Later . . .

I know if I don't write this down, I'll never get it out of me. So, I'm just going to write it as fast as I can. Just the facts. Just what happened.

On Friday I left school and walked down to Lauren's place with her and Ross. We went inside and Ross packed a bowl, and we all smoked out. Lauren made cosmos and we raided the fridge while we watched TV. Blake and Ian showed up and we all headed down to the Promenade for Mexican food. Ian has a fake ID and ordered a pitcher of margaritas. Lauren and I finished our water and Blake poured margaritas into our glasses.

I was feeling really buzzed when we got back to Lauren's and Ross was smoking more weed. I said I was getting too tired from the weed and the drinks and the food. Blake looked over at Ian and said, Well, I've got a solution to that.

Then he pulled a big bag of cocaine out of his pocket and Lauren clapped her hands. Ross and Ian said that they were staying away from the blow as much as they could, but after Blake and Lauren both did lines, we all decided that we'd just do a little bit and then go get in the hot tub on Lauren's roof.

The coke instantly perked me up and I felt so much more awake. Lauren dragged me back to her room to put on swimsuits. We must've taken a long time because Blake poked his head into her bedroom, and was like, Ross and Ian are doing another line. You girls want more?

That's the bad thing about cocaine: Even when you say you're only going to do one line, you end up doing more because it makes you feel so on point. I had been making Lauren laugh, and I felt beautiful in the little white bikini she gave me. I waltzed out into the living room in nothing but her swimsuit and Blake convinced me to let him do a line off of my stomach. I lay down on the couch, and he poured a little line of coke out right under my belly button. I was laughing so hard when he snorted it because it tickled, and then he licked the place where the cocaine had been, and ran his tongue all the way up to my breasts, then between them up to my neck, and kissed me in front of Ian and Ross.

Lauren walked in and saw us kissing, and was like, You two get a ROOM! Blake said he was fine with that idea and picked me up and threw me over his shoulder like a sack of potatoes and headed down the hall over my giggling. I tickled him until he dropped me and then we all went upstairs to the hot tub.

Lauren and Blake brought up two shakers of cosmos and plastic glasses for everybody. Lauren's hot tub on the roof is AMAZING. You can see the pier with the big Ferris wheel and roller coaster all lit up, and it was a clear night at the beach. We laughed and talked about God knows what, and Ian smoked some cigarettes because he does that when he does cocaine.

I kept sniffing and feeling the cocaine drip down the back of my throat and I realized that I kind of liked that feeling now. I remembered how weird it had felt at first, but now I could feel the buzz of the coke—making me want to talk and laugh. Coke makes everything interesting, and alive feeling, for about 20 minutes or so, and then I always want more.

Lauren went back downstairs to fill up the martini shakers again, and Blake followed her down to help out. I was trying to take deep breaths in the hot tub and just relax, which is hard to do on coke. Ross was talking about how his mom was going to have to work on Thanksgiving, but that was okay because the hotel had an amazing 5-star restaurant and he was going to get to hang out there with Ian, whose mom and dad were still in Italy.

I started feeling this weird anxious feeling in my stomach and asked Ross if he was feeling it too. He said he was, and Ian said it was because they must've cut the cocaine with something speedy. He said that some Xanax would help level out that feeling, and I remembered that the last time I'd done coke Lauren had given us Xanax.

I told the boys I'd go get us some, and I grabbed a towel. Ross whistled at me as I got into the elevator, and I blew him a kiss. When I walked into Lauren's place, I heard music coming from the speakers hidden in the ceiling and walls of the condo. Lauren and Blake weren't in the kitchen, so I walked back toward Lauren's bedroom. I saw her door was open about a foot, and I opened my mouth to call her name, but that's when I heard it: a gasp.

I've been thinking about that gasp for two days now. Wishing I would have just turned around right then, and gone back into the kitchen, and mixed another drink, and gone back up to the hot tub.

But I didn't.

I couldn't.

Maybe it was the coke, or the vodka, or both. I felt my heart start to race like a locomotive about to pound through my chest. I smelled the coke in the back of my throat, sort of greasy like gasoline, and I felt the bottom drop out of my stomach. It was fear and rage all rolled into one. My hand was shaking as I touched the doorframe, and I held my breath as I peered into the room.

I saw Blake's naked body on top of Lauren on the bed, her legs wrapped around him, her fingers running down his back, and that's when I heard the second gasp. I saw the mirror of cocaine on the bedside table, and something in me snapped. I kicked the door so hard that it slammed open and hit the wall.

And as I kicked the door, I screamed.

I cried and screamed the words that echoed in my head as Blake scrambled for his jeans, and Lauren pulled the comforter over herself, the words I repeated over and over as she cried and begged me not to be upset, the words that Ian and Ross heard me sob as they drove me home:

HOW COULD YOU?

Later . . .

Blake and Lauren have both texted me a gazillion times. Finally I turned off my phone.

Cam came home a little bit ago and poked his head in my room. He closed the door behind him, and walked over to the bed, and sat down really gently, like I was a glass of wine balanced on the pillow and might spill all over the place.

He looked at me, and then down at the striped rug that pokes out from under my bed. He told me that Lauren had texted Astrid while we were driving back.

I was silent for a second. We just sat there looking at each other. Cam could have said anything at that moment:

*I told you so.

*You're so dumb.

*What did you think was going to happen?

*Did you think he actually liked you?

But that's the thing about Cam: He doesn't care about being right. He cares about me. He reached over and took my hand, and instead of saying any of those things, he said:

I'm sorry.

Something about those words knocked me over, and I spilled out all over him. I cried, and he leaned over and hugged me and I pressed my face into his shoulder and that's how Mom found us when she came in. She wanted to know what happened, and once more I held my breath and waited for Cam to spill the beans.

But he didn't.

He just said that Lauren had been unkind to me.

Unkind.

Who talks like that? But you know what? He was right. It wasn't that I cared so much about Blake. It was that what Lauren did . . . well, it's not what friends do to each other.

Blake didn't break my heart.

Lauren did.

November 7

I am leaving for school in 2 minutes. I don't know how I'm going to make it through this day. I don't even want to SEE

Lauren, let alone TALK to her. We've eaten lunch together almost every day this school year.

How is this going to work?

Later . . .

Turns out it's not so hard not to speak to Lauren today. She walked up to me at our lockers and said, I'm sorry. I didn't look at her. I didn't answer her. I just closed my locker and walked away. She didn't even try to meet us for lunch. I walked down to the cafeteria with Ross and Cam and Astrid. Astrid gave me a hug and asked me if I was okay. I smiled and told her I would be.

But I don't think I will.

Not because of Blake, or Lauren, or what happened last Friday. It's because I feel this sense of dread in my stomach since I've sworn off drugs and drinking again. And something in my head feels like I'm going to miss out on all of the fun. Isn't that CRAZY? After everything I've gone through? After all of the bad stuff, and tears, and feeling terrible?

But it's true. I feel like I won't have anything to look forward to. The excitement about drinking cosmos with Lauren, or smoking out with Ross, or doing lines with Blake is over now. What am I supposed to do for fun? Go to movies with Mark?

I'm afraid.

Afraid this can't last.

November 11

Ross and Lauren didn't show up today. I texted Ross, but I didn't hear back from him. Of course, he's not really tied to his phone so I guess I shouldn't be surprised. Still, I can't shake the feeling that it's weird. I feel like I'm being petty and stupid, but I have this feeling in my gut that they were hanging out together all day.

ARGH. I feel like a psycho.

Ross can hang out with whoever he wants. It's not my business. I just don't want to be around Lauren anymore.

Tonight I'm helping make the shopping list for Thanksgiving. It's less than 2 weeks away. I can't wait. I love the holidays. We have my dad's whole family over for Thanksgiving, and then a bunch of Dad's college students who don't go home because the break is so short. It always feels so great to have a full house and lots of food and a big fire in the fireplace. Dad always borrows folding tables from the college and we set them up in the living room.

I'm kind of relieved that I don't have to go out with everybody tonight. I just want to go home and put on my sweats and watch TV. Maybe Mom will order pizza.

Later . . .

When I was on my way home from school with Cam, Mark texted me.

Cam asked who it was, and when I told him it was Mark, he didn't say anything for a minute. As we pulled into the driveway, he said he knew that I thought Mark was a dork, but that he was actually a really nice guy.

I just can't. I don't have the energy. I don't need a date.

I need a nap.

November 15

I was singing in choir today, and I heard Lauren's voice over the melody, and I got SO ANGRY that I wanted to march up the stairs in the choir room and SMACK HER.

After school yesterday we were both at our lockers at the same time. I've been waiting at the end of the hall until she finishes getting her books, then going to my locker so we don't have to stand there in silence while she fidgets and keeps looking at me to see if I'm still upset with her.

Like I'm ever NOT going to be upset with her.

Hello??? What planet is she on? I'm just going to MAGICALLY be okay with all of this one day?

Anyway, yesterday I just didn't give a crap and she was taking forever, texting somebody in front of her open locker instead of getting her shit and getting out of there. So, I just walked up and opened my locker and got my stuff, and closed it, and as I was walking away, I heard her say my name, and then she yelled my name, and it was like this bizarre moment where everybody sort of froze, and our little section of the hall got momentarily quiet.

I turned around and looked at her, and I could tell. I just knew: She was doing coke. Her eyes had that wide, wild stare in them, and her nose was a little red. And right as I turned around, she made a quick little sniff.

The screwed up thing is that this look passed between us where she saw that I knew.

And she gritted her teeth and blinked hard and then said, Are you just never going to look at me again?

I stood there, then I shook my head slowly, then turned and walked around the corner.

The worst thing about this is that I'd never really had a BEST friend before. Lauren was the first person I'd ever been close to like that, and as much as I know that I can't be friends with her anymore, I also MISS having a friend that close. I miss being able to laugh with her about stuff. I miss that excited feeling I got when we were mixing cosmos and how "bad" it felt and how we were partners in crime. I was also WORRIED about her. I couldn't believe that she had done a line at SCHOOL.

I mean, that's INSANE. If she gets caught, she'd be expelled and be in HUGE trouble.

I miss Lauren. But not this Lauren. I miss the Lauren I met that first night at Blake's.

I wonder if she exists anymore?

November 17

It's so weird how things change so fast. Those first couple months of school, I just assumed that we'd be one big gang the whole year. We were all together all the time. I let myself imagine how we'd all give each other Christmas presents and go to parties together, and winter formal. Hell, I let myself imagine going to prom with all of them.

Ross still sits by me in our classes, but I feel like there's this thing between us that's holding us back from being the way we used to be. It makes me SO UPSET because he was MY friend first, and now I feel like Lauren is coming between us. I mean, he doesn't really hang out with her at school or at lunch either, but he's not totally present with us on the days he joins us for lunch.

I talked to Astrid about it. She isn't really hanging out with Ross or Lauren anymore either. She and Cam go out every Saturday night, like clockwork. This week Cam wants me to come and bring Mark.

He's been following me around again.

November 20

So, Mark came with us to the movies last night. It was me and Cam and Astrid and Mark.

AND IT WAS SO BORING.

Ugh.

Cam kept smiling at me like SEE? ISN'T THIS FUN? And I tried. I reeeeeally did try. But I just can't. Mark was sweet and he even held my hand during the movie. He smells good, and he has really big arms. They stretch out the band on the sleeve of his T-shirt. He's cute.

There's nothing wrong with him.

There's something wrong with me.

I just kept thinking how much more fun the whole thing would've been if I was stoned. Or had a drink.

Now I wish I'd never EVER even taken a tiny toke off of the pipe Ross handed me. I wish I'd never laid eyes on Lauren or taken a martini glass full of ice-cold cosmos from her. I wish I'd never swallowed that hit of E or snorted that first line of cocaine.

I wish I'd never done ANY of it.

And it's not because it made me feel so bad.

It's because it made me feel SO GOOD.

And now . . .

I can NEVER not KNOW how good it feels. Now I'm trapped knowing how great it is, and not being able to do any of it.

Later . . .

Cam just came in and saw that I was writing. He thought I was doing homework. Lately I usually am because there's nothing else to do. It's not like I'm going to go hang out with Ross and get high, or go party with Lauren. My grades have been WAY better on quizzes and stuff, which is good. Cam wants to go to yoga. There's a class at 4 p.m. on Sundays that Marty teaches.

I think I'll go.

It's not a party, but something inside me feels like it's a good idea. I can't shake the feeling that maybe if I'd kept going to yoga, I wouldn't have started drinking and doing drugs. Or maybe that's crazy. Whatever.

At least it'll be something to do that isn't homework.

Later . . .

Yoga was good.

I feel more peaceful on the inside, more content, maybe. Mom and Dad wanted to know if Cam and I wanted to join them for a game of Scrabble.

SCRABBLE. Like a board game. Yes, an actual BOARD is involved. Not on an iPad, not on a laptop, like little pieces of wood, on little pieces of cardboard.

I said yes.

And usually I HATE playing word games with my dad

because he's like super-duper reader guy and knows all the vocab stuff that I have to study my ass off for.

But I think I said yes because I'd been to yoga. I felt calm. And I dunno. It seemed like a nice idea to hang out with our family.

Just us.

OH! And at yoga, I was looking at the schedule and I noticed that Ian's name isn't on the schedule for the next month ANYWHERE.

I asked Marty if Ian was taking a break, and she said that nobody had heard from him. He'd stopped coming to class, and when they called him, he said he wasn't going to teach anymore.

I started to text Ross to see what was going on, but Ross hasn't really been returning my texts. Or hanging out with us at school that much. I have this nagging suspicion that he's hanging out with Ian and probably Lauren. If that's the case, I know what they're doing. I don't have to ask.

As much as I don't want to admit it, I feel completely left out.

November 21

I just finished my last chemistry quiz before THANKSGIVING! I'm SO GLAD it's a short week this week. Lauren is in New York with her mom for the holiday. She texted me before she flew out early this morning to say that she hoped I'd have a good holiday and that she was "thankful" for me.

Whatever.

Ross asked me if we could go to lunch today. I said yes. He seemed like he wanted to talk about something. I almost asked him about Ian, but I decided not to. He can tell me if he wants.

Later . . .

Cam saw me leaving for lunch with Ross and gave me the eagle eye from down the hall. GOD. I HATE THAT. I've been the perfect student for the past couple of weeks, and he acts like I'm about to run around the corner and snort a line every time he looks the other way.

Ross and I had fun at lunch. He didn't mention Lauren. We talked about Thanksgiving, and what he usually does. This year he can't be at his grandma's in Florida with all of his cousins, so he's just going to the hotel where his mom works. I told him he'd said that he was going to do that with Ian.

He got really quiet when I mentioned Ian's name. This faraway look came into his eyes.

I hope he's okay.

(Ross. Not Ian. I mean, I hope Ian's okay too, but I care less about Ian than I care about Ross.)

November 24

THANKSGIVING!

Today was so great. Mom made us banana bread and pumpkin bread to eat while we watched the parades. Then we helped Dad move all the furniture and set up the tables in the living room. I couldn't believe that we fit everyone in there! We had 35 people eating at tables in the living room. Dad was up at 5 a.m. smoking a turkey on the grill, and Mom had one going in the oven. They had a contest to see whose would turn out the prettiest. Dad's won. Mom's tasted really great, but something about smoking it on the grill made the skin on Dad's all crispy and bronze colored, and it tasted DELICIOUS.

We all sat down to eat around 3 p.m., and I can't believe the amount of food I was able to fit inside my body. I ate like I'm going to be shot the next morning.

Okay. I have to make a confession: I DID have a drink of wine. But not a lot! Just a glass! It was a mug, actually, so Mom and Dad couldn't see. I saw Cam had swigged a little bit out of Mom's glass when he went to refill it this afternoon, and so when everybody was having coffee with their pumpkin pie, I just poured some of the leftover wine out of one of the bottles into a mug, and everyone thought I was drinking coffee.

It was so fun! I got a little warm buzz, and I felt all cozy and perfect. I mean, all of the grown-ups were drinking wine, and I'm 16. It's not like I'm a kid anymore.

Anyway. We just got back from a movie, and Dad pulled out all of the leftovers, and Mom started talking about putting up the Christmas decorations next weekend and pulled out a tin of fudge she made last night. Mom's homemade fudge is always the symbolic kickoff of Christmas. She never puts it out for dessert on Thanksgiving. She always waits until everyone leaves and it's just our family.

Cam and I are watching TV. He's texting Astrid like every 37 seconds. She's in Phoenix with her family visiting her mom's family. We are also GORGING ourselves on Mom's fudge. I think I may slip into a diabetic coma.

I AM SO HAPPY. These are the moments when I think that WOW: Maybe I do have the BEST family EVER.

It's true: I really do have a lot to be thankful for.

December 3

I had a HUGE FIGHT with Mom today. She wanted me to come with them to pick out the Christmas tree. I told her I didn't want to go, and she made it like this federal case. It was like I'd told her that I'd decided to become a stripper.

ARGH.

Then Cam came to my room and tried to talk me into it, all puppy dog eyes. I was like, LOOK! I have cramps. I just spent ALL DAY on a SATURDAY writing a paper for English. I want to have a Diet Coke and a painkiller and sit and watch TV on the couch. I don't wanna go stand in the cold while Mom makes us look at every single damn tree on the lot and then ends up buying the display tree anyway. Which TAKES LONGER because they have to retie the whole thing up.

It's not personal. I just don't want to go.

And then Cam started acting all high and mighty and talking about how I had been doing so much better, but he wonders sometimes if I've really changed, or if I'm just acting like it so that he'll get off my back.

I HATE IT when he acts like that—I mean, HE'S the one who gave me my first beer, and I've smoked pot with him like a billion times now. I couldn't hold my tongue and told him that the quickest way to make me want to take a big bong rip was to stay on my case like this.

Now he's mad at me too.

CRAP.

I guess I should just go and get it over with.

WHY IS THIS STUFF SUCH A BIG DEAL???

Later . . .

That was the most monumental waste of time ever.

One and a half HOURS.

Bought the display.

But it smells nice. And I dunno . . . there's something about Christmas that just makes you happy no matter what's going on inside of you. Like cocaine. Only it lasts for like a month instead of 12 minutes.

HA HA HA HA HA HA HA HA HA.

Omg. Lauren would think that was so funny.

ughughughguhguhgugh UGH

THESE are the moments when I really MISS her.

December 7

They should just CANCEL school between Thanksgiving and Christmas. The teachers are either COMPLETELY stressed out because they've got to do all of this stuff besides teach, or they're like CRAZY Christmas spirit FREAKS in sweaters with sparkles and jingle bells on their shoes. Our U.S. history teacher has worn a Santa Hat EVERY. FREAKING. DAY. since we got back from Thanksgiving.

I love Christmas as much as the next person, but really?

Lauren has missed two days of class every week since

Thanksgiving. Astrid said she hasn't heard from her at all. I think the only one she's talking to anymore is Ross, but Ross isn't saying anything to me about it.

Today at lunch he asked me if I was ever going to forgive Lauren.

I asked him if Lauren wanted to be forgiven.

He just shrugged and looked off like he always does.

Mom told me to invite him over for dinner next week. Cam got his boxers in a bunch about that. I told him to chill out.

December 16

I got an A on my English paper!!!

Maybe it was the good grade, or maybe it's the fact that Mom has the house DONE to DEATH, or maybe it's the lights outlining the roof of the house that Dad risked his life to hang. Whatever it is, I'm officially in the Christmas spirit. I've been CHRISTMAS SHOPPING!

EEEEEEK!

I LOVE GIVING PRESENTS!

I had exactly $147 dollars that I could spend. I got Cam a new yoga mat because his is totally gross from being sweat on all the time. I also got him one of these little terry-cloth towels cut the same size as a yoga mat to CATCH the sweat so that he doesn't have to keep rearranging his towel on the mat when we're in class.

Mom is always the hardest person to buy for because I'm never sure what she really wants, but we were shopping the other day at the new mall at the end of the Promenade, and she tried on this really cute pair of shoes that were marked down like a bazillion times to $49. They were orange satin heels with a little open toe and they looked SO CUTE on her foot—like something out of a '50s TV show. She kept looking at her feet in the mirror and talking about how fun they were. But THEN she put them BACK and went on and on about how they weren't practical and she would rather spend the money on Christmas presents blah blah blah.

SO I WENT BACK AND GOT THEM!

I was really worried that they wouldn't be there, but they were. SCORE.

Dad is easy. I think Cam and I are going to go in on a couple of records that he really wants. (Yes. Vinyl records. The kind you play on a rotating disc with a needle. Sigh.) We're also going to get him a new warm-up suit because his is looking a little worse for wear.

Ross is on his way over for dinner, and Astrid will be here too. I'm really glad that they're coming.

Later . . .

Tonight was really great. Well, not at the beginning. It started out weird because Ross made some reference to Lauren and homecoming and Cam got all bristled up and didn't talk a lot. But then Ross was telling us about Thanksgiving at the hotel where his mom works, and how the chef had come out to their table to say hello and wish them a happy holiday, and this old lady at the next table pushed her chair out into a waiter who had a bottle of wine, and the bottle hit the floor right at the chef's feet and exploded, drenching the chef in pinot noir.

Ross is hilarious when he tells stories, and by the time he was done, Cam was gasping for breath and my dad was laughing so hard he was crying.

It felt just like old times.

Well, I guess, it felt like this summer.

Funny how "old times" is only about 4 months ago.

It seems like it was a lot longer ago than that.

December 24

I love Christmas Eve.

I am sitting in the living room staring at the lights on the 9-foot Douglas fir. Dad just walked into the living room and gave me a kiss on the cheek. He turned up the lamp and said I'd go blind if I kept writing in the dark.

I remember when I was a little girl, Dad would always help Cam and me leave a plate of cookies and a glass of milk for Santa before we went to bed on Christmas Eve. I guess I was about 6 years old the year that Cam got out of bed to check and see if the cookies and milk were gone and discovered Dad eating them. He cried and cried—not because there wasn't a Santa Claus, but because there weren't any more cookies left and now Santa wouldn't come.

I didn't cry, and Cam got upset with me for not caring. Dad just winked at me and smiled as he rocked Cam back and forth. Dad knew I knew about Santa being make-believe.

I don't know how I knew.

I just always did, I guess.

I've always thought that the invisible and the imaginary are the same thing.

I guess that's why I like Christmas Eve so much. It's the one night where I feel like things that aren't seen have a possibility of existing: angels, elves, flying reindeer. It all seems possible somehow.

I've been thinking about Lauren a lot lately. She still texts me every once in a while. I mean, it's not like I don't see her. Ross calls me the Ice Queen because I haven't actually acknowledged her since that night last month.

But tonight, staring at the lights and the star at the top of the tree, I realize that I've been thinking more and more about the good parts of Lauren and the weird space that's been left in my life for the past 7 weeks without having her in it.

Who knows? Maybe the ice will melt one day. It hasn't yet, but tonight is a night about magic that makes everything feel . . .

Possible.

December 25

OH MY GOD!

MY PARENTS GOT ME A CAR!

YAAAAAAAAAAAAAAAAAAAAAAAAAAAAAAAAA AAAAAAAAAAAAAAY!

I can't even BELIEVE IT!

It's not a new car or anything. It's a Certified Pre-Owned Jetta. It's two years old, but it was at a used car dealership and it still has that NEW CAR SMELL. Dad said I'd done such a good job this fall in school and had been so responsible lately that he and Mom felt like I was ready.

THIS IS SO AMAZING!

I'm going to pick up Ross and then we're going to go get hot chocolate and see a movie.

Later . . .

I was just sitting in my car in the driveway listening to music after I dropped Ross off. I still can't believe it. I just want to be in that car ALL THE TIME!

Mom just walked through the living room in the shoes I bought her and her bathrobe. She stuck out her foot like a movie star and laughed and smiled at me.

I think she was really surprised that I was paying attention to what she wanted.

Cam and I are going to go to yoga every day this week since we're off from school. He loved his yoga mat.

January 1

I can't believe it's a new year already. Tomorrow we go back to school, and for the first time EVER I'll get to drive my NEW CAR into the parking lot.

Dad surprised Mom with a night of dinner and dancing in a supper club at the top of a skyscraper downtown. Cam got permission to go to Astrid's and Ross invited me over to dinner because his mom was having a New Year's Eve party.

When I got there, the place was already packed and Ross dragged me upstairs to his room away from all of the adults. He was totally annoyed because he wanted Ian to come over but his mom wouldn't allow it. She said that Ian is a bad influence on Ross. He said he yelled at her and said that Ian wasn't an influence, that he was a BOYFRIEND. His mom thinks that Ross is just going through a phase, apparently. Ross thinks his mom is under the impression that I want to date him, so she's always saying that he should invite me over.

I was giggling SO HARD when he told me that, partly because early on that was true, and partly because it's SO RIDICULOUS. I guess after being around Ross so much, I wouldn't want to imagine him any other way.

I asked Ross where Ian had been, and a stormcloud passed across his face. He went completely silent, and finally I just tossed myself back onto his bed and yelled REALLY? You're just not going to TELL ME?

He looked at me long and hard, then said to wait a second, he needed "supplies." Then he ran out of the room. In a minute he came back, only he was wearing a snowboarding jacket. He unzipped the coat and pulled a bottle of champagne out of the sleeve. He popped the cork and said, Happy Frickin' New Year, then took a big gulp that made the bottle foam up and spill all over him. We laughed and he grabbed a towel out of his bathroom and mopped it up.

When he handed the bottle to me, I took it, but I immediately heard an alarm go off in my brain: YOU'RE DRIVING YOU'RE DRIVING YOU'RE DRIVING.

I shook my head and reminded him that I had a car now. When I handed the bottle back to Ross, he rolled his eyes and handed it back. He said, Gimme a break. You're not going to get tanked, you're just going to have a couple sips and then I'm going to tell you about Ian.

I decided he was right.

I took the bottle.

I took a drink.

The alarm stopped.

And then Ross told me about Ian. Apparently they broke up about the same time I found out that Ian wasn't teaching anymore. Ross said that Ian had dropped out of school and stopped teaching yoga.

Then Ross got really quiet, only I could tell that he had more to say. He went over to his dresser and opened the top drawer, pulling out a little brown box. He slid off the top that was fitted so tightly it looked like a solid piece. He pulled out his pipe, packed a bowl, took a deep toke, then handed the pipe to me and waited until I put my lips to it. He sparked the lighter and I pulled the smoke through the purple glass into my mouth, then breathed it deeply into my lungs.

It didn't take very long for me to feel the floating sensation in my head, and when I opened my eyes, Ross was staring at me, smiling so sweetly. He said, You missed it, didn't you. I giggled and nodded. I said, Don't think this is going to become a habit or anything.

Ross took another couple of hits until the bowl was cashed and then he tapped out the ashes in the trash can and put the pipe back in its secret box in the dresser. Then he turned around and told me that the day he and Lauren missed school together was the last time he'd seen Ian. They'd been up all night long the night before doing blow at Blake's house. Ross said Ian had been sort of a jerk lately, making comments about how Ross owed him for all of the free drugs he was getting.

Ross said, I looked around and realized that I had school in the morning and that I wasn't going to make it. And then I realized I wasn't having fun.

He told Ian that he didn't want to do any more coke that night, that he needed to get home. Ian laughed at him and said that was fine, he could just leave.

Ross was quiet for a minute after he told me all this. Then he looked at me and asked me a question:

How could a drug be more important to him than I am?

The hurt in Ross's eyes made me catch my breath and I felt myself tear up. I gave him a long, tight hug. He buried his face in my shoulder and cried. We sat like that for a long time.

He said that Ian had texted him a few times, but Ross had

told Ian that if he was doing cocaine, Ross didn't want to be around him.

I told Ross he was smart. I told him how strong he was, and what a good friend he was being to Ian to stand up to him like that. That he'd done the right thing.

Then he looked at me and tears ran down his face, and he said, Then why does it feel so wrong?

I didn't have an answer.

January 2

I just passed Lauren in the hallway on my way to first period. I couldn't believe it. I haven't seen her in a few weeks, but that's not really that long. I don't know what happened, but she looks TERRIBLE. Her skin is almost gray, and her hair is a mess, but the most shocking thing is that she looks like she lost 10 pounds over the holidays, and BELIEVE ME when I say that Lauren did NOT have 10 pounds to lose. She looks like a skeleton.

Later . . .

I didn't mean to talk to her.

I was standing at my locker and I felt her come up next to me, in a hurry. She was in a hurry because Cassie and Bethany were following her, laughing. They've been after Cam since they were in 7th grade and he's never given them the time of day.

When Lauren showed up this year and fell in with our group, they were silently pissed. Today they broke their silence.

I heard Cassie cough the words COKE WHORE as she passed, and I felt Lauren whirl around. She told them to fuck off and Bethany stopped and said, OR WHAT? I was trapped in the middle of this, trying to look busy with my gym bag. Bethany was in full-on bitch mode. She called Lauren a druggie and when Lauren said it wasn't true, Bethany just laughed. Cassie said really loudly, We all KNOW it's true. I mean, your own best friend won't even LOOK at you anymore.

I don't know what it was, but something about that comment made me SO PISSED OFF. In a split second I realized that I was WAY more angry at Cassie Wasserman than I could ever be at Lauren. I slammed my locker so hard that I felt Lauren jump beside me. I turned around very slowly and looked at Cassie like I might decide to take a bite out of her head. Very softly and slowly I said, While we'd love to stay for more of your enlightening banter on the nature of our friendship, Lauren and I are headed to lunch. I looked at Lauren. Her eyes darted to mine as if she were afraid to look at me, like she was staring up at the sun after being locked in a dark closet for a week.

I smiled at her and jangled the keys to my car: I'm driving.

I saw tears fill her eyes, but before they could fall, I grabbed her arm and sped her outside to my car in the parking lot.

We hit the McDonald's drive-thru for fries and Diet Cokes. Then I opened the sunroof because it was a beautiful day, turned the heater on full blast because it was a little crisp, and drove toward the highway along the beach. I pulled off onto the side of the road where Ross had parked the first time that he took me surfing, and put the car in park.

Then we talked.

She told me how sorry she was about the thing with Blake. She told me he'd tried to pressure her and Ross into selling drugs for him. He'd offered them free coke, but they'd refused. Ian took Blake up on the offer, and the two of them had been selling drugs to Ian's college friends like crazy.

I asked her why she looked so awful.

She said she'd gone to New York to get away from Blake and Ian over Christmas break but that a guy she'd been dating off and on before she came out here invited her to a party on Christmas night, and he'd had an 8 ball of cocaine. She said they were awake for 2 days, and then he just kept getting more.

We sat there in silence for a while, staring at the waves. Then I reached over and took her hand. She started crying. After she stopped, she wiped her face with her free hand and squeezed my fingers tight. She thanked me for standing up for her today, that she almost didn't come back to school because she couldn't take it anymore. She said she'd thought about just getting her GED and going back to New York to start college.

I smiled at her and said, You CAN'T go to college yet. We haven't gone to winter formal and PROM!

She smiled at me cautiously. I said, But first things first: You look like SHIT.

Her eyes went wide, then we both busted out laughing. We laughed until the tears ran down our cheeks and we couldn't breathe and we were late getting to school from lunch, but I don't care.

I have my best friend back.

January 3

Astrid and Cam almost fell down when they saw Lauren and me walking toward them for lunch today. Ross broke into a big smile and said, The band's getting back together, dude. Cam was really quiet during lunch, and tonight after dinner he came to my room and said he was worried about me. He said he was afraid I would start. I threw a pillow at him.

He was all, WHAT? I'm just concerned.

I told him he had nothing to be concerned about. I mean I have MORE than proven that I can stay off drugs. I'd only had that tiny hit of pot with Ross on New Year's Eve. That's IT. Well, and a couple sips of champagne that night.

Cam reminded me about the mug of wine at Thanksgiving, and I told him that he needed to back off because I saw him swigging out of Mom's glass that day in the kitchen before he refilled it.

GOD. He can be SUCH a hypocrite.

I told him I could take care of myself.

He got this snotty tone and said he hoped so because he wasn't going to ever cover for me with Mom and Dad again. I told him he wouldn't have to. He said, I better not, then he stalked out.

GAAAAAWD! Why does he ALWAYS have to have the last word?

January 6

Lauren asked if she could come spend the night tonight. I texted Mom and she said it was fine. It's only Friday, but Lauren is already looking more normal. For one thing, I've been making her EAT! I told Ross he should come over too, and we'll order pizza and watch movies.

January 8

This weekend was just like old times, only better! I forgot how much Lauren made me laugh. We had such a good time on Friday night with Ross. We were all up until like 3 a.m. watching TV and eating leftover Christmas fudge and cookies and stuff. Cam even warmed up and hung out with us. He and Astrid had gone out for dinner, and when they came back, we were all having so much fun that Astrid called her mom and got permission to stay over with me and Lauren.

Ross got a call from Ian. We told him to ignore it, but I could tell that it bothered him. He said he wouldn't call back, but he left a little bit after that, and I'm sure he called him.

ANYWAY: We all made plans to go to the big winter formal which is the last Saturday in January.

January 13

Friday the 13th. The scariest thing about the month of January is that sometimes I feel like it will

NEVER END.

GOD. It's INTERMINABLE.

(That's the word I got WRONG on the vocab quiz today in English. SHEESH.)

January 18

Lauren and I are going to look for outfits for winter formal
after our choir sings at the chamber of commerce luncheon on
Saturday at City Hall. I can't wait. Ross said he's going to come
hear us sing. Who knows? Maybe we'll drag him along with us
to shop. He's been no help at all when we've taken him before.
He's not one of those PROJECT RUNWAY gays. He always
wants us to just buy whatever is the lowest cut, and the shortest.

He's such a perv.

January 21

Okay okay okay okay. I KNOW I said I was DONE with drugs,
but Ross had his pipe with him today, and we smoked a little.
Just a COUPLE HITS EACH.

Lauren and I found the CUTEST outfits for winter formal
today. There were racks and racks and racks of stuff at Nordstrom
marked down like 70 percent off. I guess stuff doesn't sell very
well after Christmas. Ross met us afterward at Lauren's place. Her
dad was watching a basketball game on TV, so we all went back
to Lauren's room and we tried on our stuff for Ross. I got the
cutest little black dress with sequins at the neck, and Lauren got
this silver dress that I LOVE.

After we tried on our dresses, Lauren said she wished her

dad wasn't home so she could make us cosmos to celebrate our good bargains, and Ross pulled out his pipe and wiggled his eyebrows up and down.

Both he and Lauren just turned to look at me like I was the one who had to give the okay.

I just looked at them both and said, LOOK, you losers. We can smoke pot, but we are NOT doing coke again. EVER. Or Ecstasy or anything else. And on the night of the actual dance we ARE NOT DRINKING. Because I have to drive, and if I can't drink, you two aren't drinking either. Got it?

They both nodded and then I said, JEEZ. When did I become JIMINY CRICKET?

When I said that, Lauren busted out laughing, and pretty soon we were all giggling like lunatics. Lauren put on some music and we just hung out in her room for a couple hours, smoking pot, and talking and laughing. I forgot how much fun we have when we're stoned.

Next week is going to be SO MUCH FUN.

I'm so glad we're not taking dates and stuff. Mark keeps asking me but yesterday I told him that I think we're just better as friends.

God, I hope he GETS THAT this time. I mean . . . even if we dated, would he KISS me? NO. Would he want to make out? NO. So . . . we'd be friends anyway, right? Because what fun is it to go out with a guy who won't kiss you??

January 26

I tried on my new dress for winter formal today and went to show Mom, and DAD walked into the living room and had a minor meltdown. He went OFF on how it was too short, and it looked like I was cheap and all of this complete CRAP.

Mom was trying to stick up for me and saying that she thought I looked really mature and the dress fit really well. She said that I wasn't a little girl anymore, and I was going with a group of friends, and Cam would be there, and Dad just got all red in the face and was like MARGARET, WHY ARE YOU TRYING TO TAKE HER SIDE?? And then he stomped into his study and told me that I would wear that dress to winter formal over "his dead body."

WHO SAYS THAT?

Is this like a MOVIE FROM THE '80S???

I just started BAWLING and ran into my room.

He came in later, all hanging his head and telling me that he was sorry. He said sometimes he forgets that I'm not a little kid anymore, because when he looks at me he still sees that little girl. I was really quiet as I listened, and then I told him that he really hurt my feelings because I wasn't trying to be CHEAP. I was trying to look pretty.

He just looked at me and said, To who?

January 27

Today is Friday and the dance is tomorrow, but I can't get that question my dad asked me out of my head: To who?

Who do I want to look desirable to? I mean, it would be one thing if I had a date, or even a crush on somebody. The thing that I keep thinking about over and over again is that I just want to look like Lauren. I mean, I never will because her legs go all the way up to her chin and she's like a head taller than me and has beautiful (NATURALLY) blond hair. But I want to feel like I'm as stylish as she is.

I'm wearing the dress.

January 28

Cam is picking Astrid up at her place, so Ross is coming here, and then we're going to go over to Lauren's to get ready. Mom wanted us to all come here so she could take pictures, but I was like NO. I am NOT going to have Dad FREAK OUT again because of my dress, or my makeup. Besides, the shoes I'm wearing are at Lauren's. Her dad got her these AMAZING Jimmy Choos for Christmas. Well, he gave her his Amex and SHE got these AMAZING shoes for Christmas. Like, 10 pairs. She's actually going to let me wear this pair that she hasn't even WORN YET!!!

How amazing is THAT?

Our friendship is even stronger, I think, because of what happened.

Cam texted me and was like, I want to see you at the dance as soon as you get there. I know he's afraid I'm going to drink and drive. ARGH.

I wish he'd lay off of the LAW & ORDER routine. GAWD.

Oooh! I think I just heard Ross pull up. YAY.

January 30

My whole life is a FUCKING NIGHTMARE.

I keep thinking that at any moment, I'll just wake up. Poof. Like that. It'll be easy, and all better, and none of this will have happened.

But I'm awake. I'm sitting here in my bedroom actually about to write these words in my journal:

I got a D.U.I.

Yep. I was Driving Under the Influence.

We got high at Lauren's. Ross had plenty of the "cronkest cush" as he likes to call it. We smoked until I could barely stand up on my Jimmy Choos, but we had NO cosmos. As I drove us to the school, I got a little paranoid. I'd never driven stoned before, and it was sort of stressful. I kept checking my speed, and all of the mirrors, and this guy honked at me when I was turning right. I guess he thought I was going too slowly, but I didn't care. I wanted to make sure that I didn't have a wreck or something. I was relieved when we finally got to the school and parked.

The formal was lame. Astrid and Cam were there, and they were dancing with Jason and Elizabeth, and they all went out to the bleachers on the football field to make out. Of course, at that precise instant, Mark spotted me and started walking toward us with a girl from his church who goes to this private Christian school. The girl Mark was with was pretty, but as he approached us, Mark couldn't stop staring at my legs. Ross whispered to Lauren that Mark was getting as much as he'd ever get before his wedding night right this second while he stared at me. That made me laugh right as they reached us and I think the girl from the Christian school thought I was laughing at her, which was TOTALLY AWKWARD.

When they finally walked away, I turned around to glare at Ross, who was sending a text message. Lauren looked at me and then she looked at Ross. Then she said, OMG. LET'S GET OUT OF HERE. Ross grinned up from his phone and said that he had an idea. I said I was too stoned to drive and handed my keys to Ross, who jumped behind the wheel.

Ross took side streets and drove through a beach neighborhood south of ours, then parked on the curb at the edge of a little neighborhood that has houses built along some canals. Lauren and I teetered across a little wooden bridge at the end of the sidewalk, and Ross led us through a low wooden gate and to the front door of one of the houses.

The first person I saw when we walked through the door was Blake, and I caught my breath. I hadn't seen him since that night at Lauren's, scrambling for his clothes, and I felt this stab in my chest that took my breath away for a second.

He was in the kitchen with Ian, leaning over a clear glass pie plate filled with cocaine. He was skinnier than I remembered, but he looked up at me and smiled.

Right at that moment, I knew.

I knew I'd be doing some coke that night. It's so weird, but it wasn't even a question. It was like a door clicking shut behind me. As I saw Ian bending toward the mound of white powder, every ounce of willpower I'd had in the last few months, every conversation I'd had with Cam and Ross and Lauren about not partying, just floated away.

In that moment I realized something: What I wanted, and what Cam wanted in this moment, were two different things. I WANTED to do a line. I WANTED to feel that rush. I WANTED to laugh like crazy and do another line and maybe steal one of Ian's cigarettes and have a big gulp of an icy cosmo and hear Blake tell me I looked like a billion dollars.

And you know what?

That's exactly what I did.

I marched into the kitchen where Lauren and Ross were standing looking sheepish, and Ian stood up in a flash, looking panicked like he'd been caught, and I took the straw out of his hand, and I snorted a GIANT rail as Lauren gasped, and Blake laughed, and I tossed my head back and felt the quick burn in the back of my nose, and I felt the delicious bitter taste in my mouth, and I closed my eyes and said, AAAAAAAAAAHHHH.

And then it was ON.

Lauren was making cosmos, and Blake was making passes, and Ian and Ross were making out, and BLAM: my phone exploded with text messages from Cam.

WHERE ARE YOU?

DID YOU LEAVE THE DANCE?

IF YOU'RE NOT HOME ON TIME I'M TELLING MOM AND DAD EVERYTHING.

I realized we'd been there for 2 hours, and it was almost curfew time for me: 1 a.m.

I downed my cosmo and did one more line, then I grabbed the keys from Ross and headed toward the front door and yelled, CAM PATROL! I'm heading out! Blake asked if I was okay to drive. I assured him I was. Nothing makes you more alert than coke, no matter how much you've had to drink.

Lauren came running after me, laughing, and Ross followed. I turned the key in the ignition. Ross turned up the music. I turned onto Pacific.

I felt my phone buzz in my lap. I knew it was another text from Cam. I glanced down at the screen.

Lauren screamed. Ross yelled, LOOK OUT!

BLAM!

The light had changed, and the car in front of me stopped short. We weren't going that fast, but there was a police car at the opposite corner. Suddenly there were lights and sirens, bright lights, and loud questions. The cops had flashlights, and they asked us to step out of the car.

They called a backup squad car. They put Lauren and me in one and Ross in the other. I have never felt so scared in my entire life as I did when I was sitting in the back of that car. The cuffs cut into my wrists and all I could think about was how my mom and dad were going to kill me. We all got taken to the police station and booked: Ross for marijuana possession, Lauren for underage drinking, and me for driving under the influence.

I felt like crying, but I couldn't. We were taken into the juvenile detention center, and I didn't see Ross and Lauren again until they had taken our fingerprints and our mug shots. Lauren's dad was actually the first to arrive. Ross said his mom was working at the hotel, but she showed up before my parents did because they'd been out to dinner and a play with friends.

When they showed up, it wasn't pretty. Dad was stonily silent. Mom had been weeping all the way home from the theater. Cam was waiting when we got home, and the minute we walked in the door, it started. He spilled everything:

Every drink.

Every joint.

Every snort.

Every party.

Everything.

When Mom stopped crying, she got very quiet. Dad got loud. Then he started crying, which was the WORST THING IN THE WORLD. Then Cam got an earful from both of them for not telling them what was going on sooner.

Cam turned to me and cried and said that all he wanted was for me to be happy.

Dad talked about how lucky I was that no one was hurt.

Mom talked about how lucky I was that no one had died.

Everybody kept saying that this could have ruined my life. I knew they were right. Suddenly everything that had happened, and sitting in a cell and being handcuffed, washed over me and I couldn't stop crying. I told them how sorry I was for not being the girl they thought I was, for not being the person they wanted me to be. Worse than that, I realized I wasn't the person I wanted to be. I was a criminal now. I had a police record.

Worse than that, I could've died. I could've killed someone.

I have to change.

January 31

Lauren's dad got a lawyer friend to argue her case. He's offered to have him argue for me and Ross as well. When Lauren's dad called my parents with his lawyer friend, he explained to them that since I failed the Breathalyzer test, my license would be suspended until I was 18 years old.

I'm totally screwed.

February 8

It's all over school. Cassie and Bethany have been total BITCHES to me and Lauren. Lauren keeps telling me that we'll get through it, but she's not the one whose license is suspended. She's not the one who will have to endure another YEAR of high school without a car.

Cam is really quiet around me now. He can barely look at Ross and Lauren. Mom has been checking my phone for texts or calls from Blake and Ian. I can barely text Ross and Lauren.

THIS IS A FUCKING NIGHTMARE.

I've been trapped in the house every night and the weekend

and don't get to hang out with Lauren or Ross by myself. Mom and Dad walk around like somebody has died. I just want to SCREAM and shake them and say SNAP OUT OF IT!

I can't wait to get to school tomorrow.

I can't believe I just wrote that sentence.

February 14

When I pictured the way my Valentine's Day would go this year, it never involved going to court for a DUI. I knew my license would be suspended (it was), but nobody had told me about the REST of the punishment. Ross, Lauren, and I have to do 50 hours of community service AND we have to go to two AA meetings every week for the next two months.

AA stands for "Alcoholics Anonymous," and I am mortified about having to go. I was serious about making a change and really becoming the person that I want to be, but I'm not a DRUNK. Yes, I like to have a cosmo with Lauren and Ross, and smoke a joint, or do a line every once in a while, but an ALCOHOLIC? I wanted to go back into the courtroom when I found out what that was and ask the judge, Do you REALLY think I'm a drunk? I mean, LOOK at me. My hair is FLAT-IRONED, for the love of God.

Anyway. We start AA and community service this weekend.

Later . . .

Oh, yeah.

Mark slid a valentine into my locker. It had Daffy Duck on it and reads, "I'm all QUACKED UP over U!"

Stellar.

[Rolling my eyes on paper.]

February 17

AA is so weird.

Ross and Lauren and I just sat there, staring. It's in the basement of this Catholic church around the corner from where Ross lives. Cam dropped me off and sat in the car with me until Lauren and Ross walked up. He said it was because he wanted to be supportive, but really I think it was because he was afraid I'd ditch, or get high with Ross and Lauren before we went.

Anyway, we have these little attendance sheets from the court that we have to get signed. Lauren wore tight jeans and a low-cut cashmere sweater and looked like something out of a magazine. She sidled up to this older guy who was telling people where to put the chairs when we got there and asked if he was the one in charge. He introduced himself and said that he was the secretary of the meeting. His name was Al. Lauren handed him our forms and asked Al if he would sign them. He said that was the job of the person in charge of "court cards" and that we should drop them in the basket when it was passed during the meeting.

We did.

But man, oh man, did we have to sit through a lot of talking first.

They read all this stuff out of a notebook, and by they I mean all the people at this meeting who were my mom and dad's age. It was so weird. They'd see us and smile really big like it was SO GREAT that we were there and then come running up and introduce themselves and shake our hands. Then they'd say WELCOME! KEEP COMING BACK.

Ross told one of them, Oh, I will be so I can get this court card all filled up.

Anyway, the stuff they read out of the notebook was all this stuff about AA not being a religion, but then they all said a prayer together about having the strength to accept things and the courage to change things. Then this woman who must've been my grandma's age got up and talked about her life for 20 minutes. This woman used to keep a bottle of scotch in her GLOVE COMPARTMENT. She said she was late for her own wedding because she was drunk. By the end, her husband left her and her kids still don't talk to her.

But then the weirdest thing happened: She started crying

with this big smile on her face and she talked about how AA had saved her life. She said she'd met some woman who helped her work the steps (whatever that is) and that she had found a higher power that helped her stay sober because she couldn't do it on her own.

Then, after she was done speaking, they passed a basket around. They said there are no dues or fees for attending AA, but if you feel like it, you can give a couple bucks, and they use it to pay the church rent for letting them meet there. Most people put a dollar or two in the basket, and we all put in our court cards. Turns out they don't hand them back to you until AFTER the meeting. (TRICKY! That way you have to STAY for the whole thing.)

After the basket was passed all these people shared all sorts of things, mainly about how they either wanted to drink and didn't that week because they called somebody at the meeting, or because they prayed and the urge went away, or they read something in this blue book that everybody had called The Big Book, and it spoke to their heart and gave them the strength not to pick up a drink.

Afterward we finally got our cards and walked outside. Mom was supposed to come pick me up, but she'd texted me during the meeting that she was running 15 minutes late. I called Mom and told her we were done and that I was walking over to Ross's apartment. She said she was on her way and would pick me up there.

We went up to Ross's room, and Lauren said that she didn't know if she could take another 15 AA meetings. I said it was the most religious nonreligious meeting I'd ever been to. Ross lit a bowl and passed it around to us.

And there was this weird thing that happened. As I reached for the pipe, I realized that I had this URGE to smoke weed. (And probably do whatever else I could.) I thought about what that lady said, about the urge being removed. I wondered if this was the urge she was talking about.

But it couldn't be, right? I mean, I'm not drunk every day. I'm not a mess. I haven't lost a husband, or been late to my own wedding. I mean, I'm not even 17 yet. This isn't even alcohol. How could I be an alcoholic?

I took a long, slow hit on the pipe and passed it to Lauren. She smiled and laughed and said that THIS was her idea of serenity.

God. What a way to spend a Friday night.

February 19

Lauren and Ross and I had to pick up trash on the side of the highway for 8 hours yesterday. It was my entire Saturday. I have to do homework all day today.

It. SUCKED. By the end of the day we were so bored and so tired that we all got kind of grouchy and stopped talking to one another.

I can't believe we have to do that for the next four weeks.

I'm so jealous that Ross got to go home and smoke pot.

February 24

I can't take it anymore. I just can't. Mom and Dad are treating me like a PRISONER. Cam is trying to "help" by taking me places with him and Astrid, as if I need a babysitter. I have to go to another AA meeting, and Mom is taking me this time. She said she wants to sit in on the meeting and see what's going on. So, of course, we won't get to go to Ross's tonight to smoke pot afterward. Or at least I won't. Lauren and Ross will, I'm sure.

February 25

Community service SUCKS. Today we picked up trash on the beach. It was FREEZING. We have to wear these little orange vests and we have these sticks to stab the trash and put it into bags. After lunch they moved us down onto one of the pedestrian bridges that takes you over the highway along the coast down to the beach. We had to scrub and paint over graffiti.

We were almost done when I saw a car pull up, and Ross said, Hey. That's Ian.

Lauren sauntered over to the window as Ian rolled it down and grinned out at us. Lauren talked to him for a second before our supervisor yelled at her to get back to work.

When she came back over, Ross asked her if she knew Ian was coming. She smiled and said that she'd texted him and that she had a surprise for us as soon as we were done. When we finished painting the wall, they took us back to the check-in office where my dad was going to pick me up. Lauren grabbed my hand and said, You better go to the restroom before you go home. She pressed a little plastic square into my hand and closed my fingers around it.

I knew what it was before I even looked. I was standing there holding a tiny bag of cocaine. Everything in my head screamed DON'T DO IT. But it was like my body couldn't resist. My heart was racing and I could hear the blood pounding in my ears. The excitement was delicious. Ross whispered that I should hurry, and I did.

I went to the bathroom and locked the stall door behind me. I poured a tiny pile of the white powder out of the Baggie onto the top of the toilet paper dispenser. Then I reached into my pocket and rolled up the receipt from the salad I'd bought at lunch. I stuck one end of the roll into my nose, held the other over the little pile of powder, and sniffed. The sniff echoed in the bathroom, and I flushed the toilet before I sniffed again, just in case anyone was listening.

When I came back to where Ross and Lauren were standing, I saw my mom had pulled up. I hugged Lauren and slipped the Baggie back into her pocket. Mom got out of the car and asked Lauren and Ross what they were doing for dinner. They both shrugged. Mom told them to come over to our place at 7.

As we drove home, Mom looked at me and said that she thought I'd been doing really well with all of this, and that she was fine with Lauren and Ross being my friends as long as we hung out at our place.

I feel SO GUILTY now that Mom is trying to be so nice to me, and I was sitting there, high on cocaine! She was telling me what a good job I've been doing, and I'm just a total fraud! I have to tell Lauren and Ross that I'm not doing it anymore, but every time they have it around me, it's the ONLY THING I can think about.

March 1

I think I'm afraid of being bored. Actually, it's not so much boredom I'm afraid of. It's that I'm afraid of not having anything to look forward to. Getting to hang out with friends used to be enough. Then I met Lauren and Ross and it was hanging out with COOL friends who I could party with. It's the excitement I miss. I miss knowing that Friday night we'd have cosmos. This guy in AA the other day said he'd been a periodic binge drinker. He used to go weeks and weeks without drinking and then he'd just get HAMMERED. I mean, that's what I did, I guess. I just don't know what's so wrong with it.

Besides the obvious, I guess? I mean, I did get a DUI.

AAARGH.

I just want to get drunk and smoke pot and do some blow with my friends and have it not be like this HUGE deal. My life wasn't RUINED. If I hadn't checked that text from Cam, no one would have even KNOWN about all of this.

I mean, I really DO want to have a good life. I want to be able to go to college, and maybe even grad school. (Dad's always going on and on about grad school.) But I'm not ready to NEVER DRINK AGAIN. I mean, my God, I'm not even in college yet, and what fun will college be if I can't drink and smoke pot?

THAT'S WHAT COLLEGE IS FOR! You work hard, you study hard, and you get to go to lots of parties and have a lot of fun. Every movie ever made about college is all about that.

I just feel so torn on the inside. I know that this hurt my family. I'm just not sure why. I mean, what does it matter to them if I decide to drink and snort some cocaine?

Speaking of colleges, we're going to look at Cam's college

next week over spring break. Lauren is going to New York for the week.

She's so lucky. I bet she's going to have a WILD time.

March 10

Dad is making this trip to Cam's college like a mini vacation. After we spend the weekend at the college, we're going to a really nice hotel. Cam likes the college. Yay.

UGH! Why can't I get excited about anything?

March 12

Cam got to sit in on some classes today and go to a soccer practice. He's all jazzed, and I can totally see how he's going to LOVE it here. I haven't seen him smile this much in a long time.

Astrid is with us, and she's thinking about coming to school here too. Although, I don't think her parents are wild about her moving. They want her to stay close and go to a college nearby. Cam says her mom thinks she is "following a boy."

SEE? That's what I'm talking about.

Why do moms and dads always get so worked up about stuff like that? SO WHAT if Astrid wants to "follow a boy" to college. WHO CARES? I mean, she's going to college, right? So what does it matter? I'm going to go to college too. It's not going to hurt if I smoke a little weed, right?

Speaking of, there are TONS of weed shops up here. They are called "medical marijuana dispensaries" and the state has made it legal to get a PRESCRIPTION for marijuana. I knew that because I heard Ross talking about it with Ian and Blake one time, but I've only seen an actual store once.

While Cam was at soccer practice, Astrid and Mom and I went shopping at some of these cute little places in Berkeley, and we must have walked by 5 places where you could buy either pot, or pipes and bongs, and other stuff.

It made me miss Ross. He'd LOVE it up here.

I texted him a couple of pictures from my phone, but I haven't heard back yet. He said he was going to spend his spring break sitting in the hot tub at the hotel where his mom works. I'll bet he's getting BAKED in his truck before he does . . .

Lucky.

March 17

This has been a really exciting week.

I know.

It's not what I expected to write, either. I just realized that I've been having a lot of fun with Cam and Astrid, and even Mom and Dad. And I didn't have any drugs to look forward to, or drinking. In fact, I barely thought about that at all after we left the college.

Excitement without drugs. Who knew? I've looked forward to stuff every day!

We went to these AMAZING museums this week. There was an exhibit at one about the history of fashion and I couldn't stop looking at it. The museum was in this beautiful park, and I wandered around looking at the plants and trees. Then we drove over the bay on a bridge that was so beautiful it gave me goose bumps.

As I stood there, staring out at the water, the sun broke through the clouds and glinted into my eyes. I squinted at the fire-colored arches of the bridge as an idea tried to take shape in my head: college, fashion, the museum. Something about this place feels right. I don't know what it is. I could imagine going to work at that museum. Do they have a graduate degree for that? I should ask my dad.

I texted Ross and Lauren a picture of me with the bridge in the background. Lauren texted me right back: SOOOOOOOOOOOO GR8!!!!!

I am still laughing about that. Usually she's the one who takes forever to respond. It's weird that I haven't heard back from Ross at all.

Tomorrow we drive back home. I guess I'll call Lauren when I get there. Usually I don't look forward to a car ride that long because reading or writing, or even playing around on my phone, makes me a little carsick. I wish I had some of Lauren's Xanax.

Oh well.

At least Astrid is here. She's been really fun to talk to. Cam has been less crazy, too, probably because I'm not hanging out with Lauren and Ross. This has been a fun time. I keep thinking about college and the museum. I'm not sure what it is, but something about that place made me feel so good, so peaceful on the inside. I kind of wish I could go there every day.

March 18

Lauren just finally went to sleep.

Oh. My. GOD.

This is fucking crazy.

We got back home, and Lauren was at my place hanging out on the front porch, which is fine, I suppose, except she's never done that before. She gave my mom this big hug, and then me and Astrid. Mom was all happy because she worries about Lauren sort of being by herself all the time, so she was happy that Lauren was there, and even though she was tired from the trip, she insisted that Lauren stay and have dinner and even invited her to sleep over and go to school with me tomorrow.

The minute we were all inside, I grabbed Lauren by the

elbow and pushed her up the stairs to my bedroom. I could tell she was H-I-G-H.

But it was weird. It didn't seem like it was a coke high.

Because it wasn't.

She was on METH. Fucking CRYSTAL METH. Her eyes were all darting around and she wasn't making a lot of sense. I got Mom to let us order pizza. Told her we had to study for a big chemistry test. Luckily Astrid had already headed home so she wasn't around to verify.

I got back to my room after I ordered the pizza and closed the door behind me. Lauren had one of my dresser drawers open and was organizing and refolding all of my T-shirts. While we were waiting for the pizza to come, Lauren told me all about it. Her ex-whatever in New York had started dealing meth. Lauren had always been really snobby about it. She said she'd always laughed at people who did meth because they were poor and meth was cheap and dirty and cooked up in a trailer.

But they were out of coke one night in New York, and so she tried it. She told me she tried to snort it, but it burnt like hell, so she smoked it out of a pipe, and she said it was amazing. She got so high on just a little bit of smoke, and it lasted for a LONG TIME. Hours instead of minutes. She said it made you feel like you were alert and awake like coke, only less happy, more warm and safe and secure. And like cleaning.

Luckily she'd taken some Xanax. I texted Ross and told him to get over here QUICK with some weed because Lauren needed some help coming down. NOTHING. I was starting to get worried, so I texted Ian and asked if he'd heard from Ross because I hadn't. I found some Tylenol PM in the medicine cabinet in Mom and Dad's bedroom and forced Lauren to take two with a slice of pizza that I had to almost shove into her mouth so she would eat it. She kept laughing and saying she wasn't hungry.

Then we watched two movies, and she finally started to doze off.

March 19

Lauren is still zonked out. I have to wake her up soon so that we can take showers and get to school on time. I'm sort of exhausted. I didn't sleep very well last night thinking about Lauren doing meth. Part of me wants to try it, but I know that it's one of the most addictive drugs that there is. I mean, I've seen all of the videos in health and read all of the pamphlets and the warnings. The police come and talk to us about it every year. They show us picture of people with TERRIBLE acne and abscesses who are delusional. None of them look like Lauren, that's for sure.

But I wonder how long it will take for Lauren to start to look like them?

And if Lauren does it, I don't know if I can say no.

Sometimes I think I'm just not a very strong person when it comes to drugs and drinking. Fuck. That's a really scary thought, and now I'm crying.

I'm going to talk to Lauren about it. I'm going to tell her that if she doesn't stay off crystal, we can't be friends.

Later . . .

I'm sitting in U.S. history. I had The Talk with Lauren. She started crying immediately and saying, I know, I know, and promising that she would never do it again. She hugged me so tight that it almost hurt, and she begged me to help her. She said she needed my help.

I told her I would help her; that we'd go to AA and actually talk to some of the people there about it. I was scared enough to actually get one of those blue books and read it. She nodded and said that was a good idea. She was crying and said that she knew this was her last chance, that none of the other girls at school would even look at her and that if she lost me as a friend again, she couldn't handle it.

I hugged her and said: Then stay off of crystal.

I haven't seen Ross this morning, which isn't that big a surprise. He's been late a lot this semester. But it's totally weird that he hasn't texted me or anything. I have this sick feeling in the pit of my stomach that he and Ian got back together.

March 20

It is 4 a.m. on a Tuesday, and I am high on meth.

I didn't meant to be.

But I am.

I'm not tired at all. I feel like I could go to school and take a test right this second. I feel good, and in control, and really . . . peaceful, somehow. I feel like everything is going to be just fine.

Ross finally called me back after school yesterday. He asked if he could come over. I said yes, mainly because I wanted to talk to him about Lauren, but also because I was hoping he'd have some weed on him, which he did.

When he came in, we said hi to my parents who were headed out to dinner with friends, then a concert series at Dad's college. Thank God they were. And thank God Cam was over at Jason's. He's spending the night over there, working on some project they have due next week.

We went to my room, and I was talking to Ross about Lauren and how she'd been doing crystal, and he asked if I wanted to smoke some weed. I didn't think it would be that big a deal.

But it was. Once we were really stoned, Ross looked at me and said, I need to tell you something.

He said that he was bored during spring break. When Lauren

got back, she called him and said she was over at Ian's place. She and Ian kept texting him to come over, so he finally did. He said that when he got there, Blake was there too, and all of them were smoking meth. Ross said he almost turned back around and walked out the door but that something in him wanted to try it. Ian told him meth would make him feel like a god.

Ross said, I just needed to try it. Just once.

It was so great that he smoked it for 4 days. He said that the sex was incredible—the best he'd ever had.

My heart was racing as he told this story. I felt the tremble in my knees and the sweatiness in my palms return. The old excitement was back, and even before he finished talking, I knew I had to try it too.

When I told him, he smiled and pulled out a clear glass pipe about the size of a pencil, but a little wider. Carefully, he took three tiny pebbles from a little plastic Ziploc bag and placed them in the end of the pipe. Then he took out a special silver lighter and flipped open the top. A blue flame sparked to life, but this was not the flame from a regular lighter. It was a steady burning flame that was hotter. He held the flame under the pipe until the rocks at the end melted into liquid, then bubbled slightly and boiled into a white vapor. Ross carefully sucked the white vapor out of the glass tube, then held it and exhaled.

The smell was acrid and chemical. Not skunky like pot, but sharp and toxic.

He held the pipe out to me, and I carefully placed the end in my mouth while he held the lighter. As the smoke filled the tube, I inhaled.

The taste was bitter and metallic. My mouth and eyes watered as I held the smoke in my lungs. Then I exhaled.

We both did this again.

And by the time I took the second hit . . .

I understood.

Ross texted Lauren after I smoked, and she was there within minutes, it seemed. I can't really be sure. She came armed with painkillers and muscle relaxers, which she said would help us go to sleep when the time came. Eventually they both went back home, but the time to sleep never came.

I've never felt so sure of myself as I do right now on this drug. I feel this level of certainty and safety that I've never possessed before. I feel like I could easily explain why this was the best choice I could've made to anyone who asked: Cam, Mom, Dad. I feel like even questioning my judgment would be foolish.

I feel like THIS was how I was MEANT to feel: confident, perfect, beautiful, sexy, in control, smart, and more certain of myself than ever.

I was grinding my teeth a little, and Lauren told me that's just an effect of the speediness of the drug. She told me to take half of a muscle relaxer or a little bit of Xanax.

I heard Mom and Dad come home several hours ago, around 11:30 p.m. I turned off my lights and crawled under the covers in my bed. Dad peeked his head in my door, and I pretended to be asleep.

But I don't need to sleep tonight.

I don't want to miss a single moment of how I feel.

Later . . .

Ross and Lauren and I left campus for lunch before Astrid and Cam could find us. We piled into Ross's pickup truck, and he drove toward Venice. I didn't even have to ask why. Ian was happy to see us. He said Blake had just been by. We hung out for about a half hour, and he gave us each a small hit of meth, just so we could get through the day at school in case we started to feel tired.

It's so funny, sitting here in class, high as a kite, but hearing everything and watching everyone around me. No one knows that I'm high. No one even suspects it.

I'm just following Ian's instructions: Talk as little as possible. It's when you start talking that people might be able to tell.

Later . . .

It's almost midnight, and I finally feel just a little bit tired. Not really sleepy, but I can tell my body needs to rest. I took a muscle relaxer that Lauren gave me. It seems to be helping a little bit.

I'm only sad that this feeling has to end.

I'm going to lie down and close my eyes to see if I can sleep.

March 21

Today sucks.

I slept for about 5 hours, and when I woke up, I felt like the underside of my shoe. My head hurts and I was so groggy I could barely talk. Mom said I looked pale and put a hand on my forehead to see if I had a fever.

Something about the way she did that just made my skin crawl. I told her I was FINE. I could tell I hurt her feelings when I snapped at her, but Cam was sitting across the table giving me the damn stink-eye. I can tell he thinks something is up.

Oh. My. GOD. This day cannot end soon enough.

Lauren isn't here, and Ross was about 10 minutes late. He said he wouldn't have come except his mom is off today and the only thing worse than being at school is being at home with her. We're walking over to Lauren's at lunch.

Later . . .

Ross smoked us out at lunch, so I feel softer around the edges somehow, a little less like I've been hit by a dump truck. I still don't know how I'm going to make it through the rest of the day. Ugh. Now I'm in this weed haze and I feel miserable. I'm not sure what I liked about pot before. It seems like such a lame high next to Tina.

LOL. That's what Ian calls crystal: Tina.

He texted Ross and told him that he should have the girls over this weekend because his friend Tina was coming.

March 22

School has been a complete fog for the past few days. I barely passed our chemistry test on Tuesday. I was stoned, and sore, and hadn't even studied. I've never made a D on a test before. Something in me doesn't care. I hear this voice in my head say that I should care, but I just don't.

I went home yesterday after class and crawled into bed and went to sleep. I slept until about 10 p.m. and wandered into the living room while Dad and Mom were watching TV. Mom jumped up and reheated some chicken soup she'd made me earlier. She asked if I was okay and said she'd thought about waking me up for dinner but wanted to let me sleep because she knew I was fighting something off.

Can you imagine if I told her I was fighting off meth?

The soup was delicious, but I still felt like I was moving under Jell-O. After I ate, I curled up on the couch with her and Dad. Mom put her arm around me, and I closed my eyes on her lap. There was something so peaceful about it. I felt like a little girl again, like I didn't need to worry about anything. It made me miss being little. It made me wonder who I was growing up to be. My eyes were closed, but they filled up with tears, and I got a big lump in my throat. When I got up to go back to bed, there was a wet spot on the throw Mom had spread across her lap.

She looked up at me and asked if I was sure I was okay. I wanted to shake my head and let it all out. I wanted to tell her everything, and crawl back onto the couch and bury my face in her lap again and let her keep me safe.

But I'm not a little girl anymore.

So I nodded and kissed her good night.

Now I'm sitting in American government, and I can't pay attention. We just took a quiz that I knew about 4 answers on. I'm pretty good at guessing, but I don't think Ross did as well.

Later . . .
Cam and Astrid came to lunch with us. They brought Mark with them.

A-W-K-W-A-R-D.

Lauren and Ross and I had to keep kicking each other under the table to keep from laughing. Every time Mark opens his mouth, he just sounds ridiculous.

It's weird having had the experiences I've had now and hearing people talk who haven't. It's like they wouldn't be able to even FATHOM some of the shit I've done.

When I was in the bathroom after lunch with Lauren, Cassie and Bethany came in to reapply their eyeliner as is their custom every other class period. When they walked by us on the way to the sink, Bethany groaned and said, Burnouts, under her breath.

Before I knew what I was doing, my hand jetted out and grabbed her blond ponytail and pulled her backward. She shrieked like she was being boiled in oil. I pulled her head back toward my mouth, and very quietly I said, Shut up, Bethany.

Lauren snorted with laughter, and Cassie got all sputtering and flummoxed, and said, Well, SCREW YOU! Really loudly. I said, You'd probably like that because nobody else has, that's for sure. Then Lauren and I walked out.

God, I hate most girls my age.

Later . . .

Ross just texted me and Lauren that he's skipping school tomorrow to go hang at Ian's. Lauren said I should go to school with Cam and then come to her place instead of going to class.

I can't take another day like today. I need to feel good again. Screw AA. Screw community service.

I'm going.

April 1

I'm writing this in a new notebook.

I'm writing this in a new city.

It's Sunday now. I'm a couple of hours away from home, a little town out in the desert.

When I woke up on Thursday, I wasn't sure where I was. Turns out I was on the psych floor at the hospital. They wouldn't give me anything to write with. They were afraid I was going to stab a pen into my throat or something. Or probably stab it into somebody else's throat. Apparently I had been unconscious for a day and a half. When they finally let my parents come in to see me, my hands were still in restraints. I'd been scratching off my skin, and fighting the nurses and orderlies.

I finally started to piece it together. A week ago last Friday, I remember walking to Lauren's. She had mimosas ready when I arrived. They were delicious—orange juice with champagne. We finished the bottle, then she drove us over to Ian's. Blake and Ross were there already, and when we walked in, Blake said he had a surprise for us.

Blake took us up to Ian's bedroom. It had a pretty view of

the canals out the window, and Ross was already standing on the balcony outside in the spring sun smoking a cigarette. There was a tray lying on the bed with a pipe, a big Baggie of meth, a lighter, and a pile of syringes with orange plastic caps.

When Lauren saw the syringes, her eyes got big and she got quiet. She looked at Blake and said, For fuck's sake. Are you kidding me?

But I saw them, and I knew. I felt the queasy feeling leap into my stomach. My mouth flooded with the metallic taste of meth. I wanted it again. That feeling. I didn't cut school for the same old feeling. I wanted it different.

I wanted MORE.

Are those for shooting up Tina?

When I said the words, everybody's head turned at once, and Blake smiled at me.

Why, yes, they are, he said.

Before anybody could move, Ross stretched out on the bed next to Blake and pulled up his sleeve. Lauren rolled her eyes and said, Oh my GOD. I HATE needles.

Ross just said, Whatever. You've done it before.

Lauren froze. I just looked at them both. Ross was staring out the balcony door. He had made a fist and shook his outstretched arm. C'MON DUDE. LET'S DO THIS.

Blake smiled. Ian held a spoon with its handle bent and

filled it with crystal meth, then held a lighter beneath it until it was liquid. Blake pulled the orange cap off of a syringe, sucked the meth up into it, then he held it in his teeth while he swabbed Ross's arm with an alcohol pad. Carefully he eased the needle into a vein. Ross flinched and then closed his eyes as Blake pushed the plunger on the syringe, then pulled it out, recapped the needle, slid it into a small coffee can on the bedside table, and said, Who's next?

I turned to Lauren and asked, You've done this before?

Ian just laughed. I realized he'd already shot up. He said of course they had. Where did I think they'd been when they missed school those days since I'd walked in on Lauren and Blake?

I knew one thing for sure in that moment: I would not be left out again.

Ross opened his eyes with a loopy smile and quietly said, Hell, yeaaaaah.

Ian walked over and squeezed in behind him at the headboard of the king-size bed. He bent over and kissed him long and hard on the lips. He smiled and said, Feel good, mister?

Ross focused his eyes back on me and said, Better than good. I'm freaking Superman.

I rolled up my sleeve. Lauren just looked at me, then shook her head.

I said, Lauren. I want this. I'm not getting left out again.

Blake got everything ready and told me to make a fist. I did, and he tapped around on my arm, then took an elastic strap and tied it around my arm near my shoulder and told me to squeeze my fist harder. I looked down and saw a light-blue spiderweb of veins start to pop up from the bend at my elbow.

The alcohol swab was cold.

The prick was fast.

As Blake pushed down the plunger, I heard bells. I kid you not. BELLS. INSTANTLY. Some people will tell you that it takes a while, but not for me. At that moment I was the sexiest, smartest, funniest, most powerful, amazing person in a perfect universe that I created. I felt the tension drop out of my shoulders, and I lay back on the bed, laughing. The sensation was instant, and delicious, and I knew right then and there that everything was warm and perfect, that everything had always been perfect, that everything would always be perfect.

Everything else comes in snapshots.

Lauren finally agreeing, and Blake shooting her up.

Running along the canals with Ross.

Taking my shoes off at the beach with Ian.

Finding Blake and Lauren naked in Ian's bed. Laughing and joining them.

Feeling Blake's body and Lauren's body and my body warm and naked and perfect.

Seeing my phone across the room, ringing and ringing. The text messages flashing across the screen: CAM CAM CAM CAM MOM MOM CAM DAD DAD DAD CAM MOM MOM MOM CAM HOME HOME HOME DAD CAM MOM . . .

I guess we were there at Ian's for a long time. Days. The nurses in the psych ward really wouldn't tell me much, just that I was checked in on Sunday, one week ago today. I finally came to around Wednesday. I was released from the hospital early this morning, and Mom and Dad walked me to the car in the hospital parking deck. We stopped at home so that I could pack a bag. Mom told me I'd be leaving town for a month. Dad told me he had my cell phone for now, and that I couldn't call, text, e-mail, or even leave a note for Lauren or Ross.

Cam came into my room as I zipped my suitcase and sat down on the bed next to me. I asked him what happened.

He said that Mom and Dad called the police when he got home from school on Friday night and no one had seen me. He said that the police told Mom and Dad they had to wait 24 hours. Cam was sure we were at Blake's and had driven up to Malibu with Astrid to check. He'd also gone to see Ross's mom at the hotel. She didn't think it was any big deal, as Ross was usually pretty much on his own.

By Sunday morning Cam was sure I was with Ian somewhere, but he'd never been to Ian's place, so he didn't know where he lived. That's when he went to the yoga studio and explained the situation to Marty. She looked up Ian's address in the computer at the studio and gave it to Cam.

Cam raced back home to tell Mom and Dad he'd gotten Ian's address and we needed to go over there, when his phone rang and it was Ross calling him. He said that when he picked up, Ross was hysterical. Crying and shouting. He kept yelling SHE'S DYING. SHE'S DYING.

Cam started crying while he was talking, slow tears flowing out the corners of his eyes as he soldiered through the story. Calling an ambulance, giving them the address, certain I'd be dead before they arrived. He said, I really thought I'd never see my little sister again.

I asked him why Ross thought I was dying.

He looked at me and said, You don't remember, do you?

I shook my head.

April 2

I'm at a rehab in Palm Springs. It used to be a motel that was built back in the '60s. The rooms are all centered around a swimming pool. Sounds nice, I guess. I wish it felt nice. I went to my first meeting today. The rules are strict. Up at 7 a.m. I have to make my bed, then report to the kitchen for breakfast. Afterward we all have chores, then group therapy starts at 10 a.m. and goes until 11:30.

It's part 12-step meeting, part counseling. I'm the youngest person here. There are mainly gay guys, one grandma who got busted cooking meth in her mobile home, and two girls who used to be strippers.

We have lunch next, then more chores, an hour of free time, then another group session. After dinner, we all load up in a big gray van and go to an AA meeting someplace in the city.

April 3

I had an individual session with the therapist at the rehab this morning. He had a mirror that he handed me and asked if I knew how I got the scratches on my face.

I've been putting some ointment on them that Mom gave me when they dropped me off. The scratches on the right side are deep, and hurt when I roll over in the night accidentally. I'm really worried they're going to scar.

I told him that I don't remember.

He said it was from the heroin.

I told him that I didn't do any heroin.

The he handed me a photocopy from a file folder he had in his hand. He said it was the toxicology report of what was in my system at the hospital. He said that the paramedics had wheeled me in dead, pumping air through my lungs with one of those squeeze thingies like you see on the emergency room shows. They gave me the highest amount of epinephrine you could give someone, and then shocked me twice before my heart started again.

The word "heroin" was circled on the report.

Later . . .

I was cleaning the toilet in my bathroom for inspection and I had a sudden flash. I don't know when it was, but I saw Blake grinning at me and saying, This is even BETTER than Tina. Don't worry. You'll love it.

I don't remember anything else.

April 5

I didn't have time to write yesterday because I had to go to the doctor for a checkup during free time. I am so pissed that they make you keep your lights off at night. I can't really sleep and I wish I could write in my journal.

I don't really know how I feel about being here. I said that in group this morning.

Randy, the counselor who runs group, said that was okay. That the reason we're here is to start feeling better.

I told him I didn't know if I felt bad.

He said, No, no. I mean we're here so that we start FEELING better; feeling EVERYTHING better. Right now, you don't know what you feel. We're here to get you in touch with what you're feeling.

April 6

I don't know if I can take it here anymore. I still feel like a zombie. Last night I woke up having bad dreams and cold sweats. I dreamed that Lauren and Ross were out by the pool. They were trying to get me to sneak out with them, and when I finally did go out by the pool, Blake was there, holding a scalpel. He had a big grin on his face and he kept saying, IT WON'T HURT! IT WON'T HURT.

I sat up in bed, panicked and sweating. I went into my bathroom and turned the water on in the shower as hot as it would go, then I sat down in the tub and cried for a really long time.

This all feels so hopeless.

What am I doing here?

Later . . .

I told the group about my dream today. Randy said that it sounded like I was feeling BETTER. I got SO MAD when he said that. I started crying, and I yelled I FEEL LIKE SHIT!

He just said, But you can feel that. Your feelings are starting to work again.

I told him I didn't want to feel the bad stuff better. That I just wanted to feel GOOD.

He said that's the tricky part about feeling better. You don't get to pick what you feel, you only get to start feeling it. All of it.

Later . . .

The weirdest thing happened tonight at the AA meeting we go to in town. This girl who was maybe only a year or two older than me spoke. She talked about all of this stuff that I TOTALLY related to. Her name was Amy, and she was the first person I ever heard speak at an AA meeting who said anything that remotely sounded like me.

This girl TOLD MY STORY!

She was 14 years old and a freshman in high school when she and her friend started drinking. Then smoking pot. Then doing Ecstasy. Then doing coke. Then doing meth.

She talked about how all of these things made her feel in

control, and pretty, and confident, and happy, and like she had something to look forward to.

Eventually she said she was shooting meth and then shooting heroin.

She ended up going to juvenile hall and being locked up there for 6 months. While she was there, she started going to an AA meeting they held, and she got a sponsor who walked her through the 12 steps. She said that she didn't really believe in a "capital G" God, but that her "higher power" was the accountability that she'd found in the rooms of AA. She said that even if you didn't believe in a god or a higher power, you could still come to AA and you didn't have to drink or use just for today, no matter what.

I think my mouth must have been hanging open, because she came up and talked to me afterward. She gave me her phone number and her e-mail address. I told her that I didn't have a phone right now because I was at the rehab.

She smiled and said that she went to that rehab too. She said she'd see if Randy would let her come visit me.

For some reason when she said that, I started crying.

Then this girl named Amy who I don't even know hugged me. She whispered into my ear, Let us love you until you learn to love yourself.

I hope she comes to visit.

April 10

I'm so excited! Amy actually came to visit me today. She said that Randy was glad she wanted to come and talk with me. During our free period, we lay out by the pool. She's one year older than me and is graduating from high school next month. Then she told me that she was going to the college where my dad works this fall to study to be a music teacher. When I told her my dad runs the music department at that college, she was like NO WAY. She'll have my dad for a class next fall!

Amy said I should watch out for little coincidences like this. She said some people in AA call them "God shots." When I laughed, she said, Yeah. That's kind of silly. I just like to think of it as all things working together for good.

Before she left, I asked Amy to be my sponsor in AA. I don't really know what all that means, but I know that you're supposed to have somebody to show you how to work the steps and to check in with if you feel like drinking or doing drugs. I'm not even really sure that I'm an addict yet, but I feel like most teenage girls probably don't get DUIs and then overdose on heroin and end up in rehab.

I know that in a couple of weeks we have "Family Day" coming up, where Cam and Mom and Dad will come down and I'll have to talk to them about all of this. I'm not sure what I'm supposed to say. When I think about it, I get that nervous feeling in my stomach. I feel so guilty and so ashamed that I've put everyone through this.

The first step in AA says, "We admitted we were powerless over alcohol—that our lives had become unmanageable." Amy said that I could substitute any drug I wanted for the word alcohol if that made it easier to understand. She also said that overdosing and getting a DUI and being high on crystal at school sounded pretty unmanageable to her.

And you know what we did when she said that?

We laughed! 'Cause it was like the UNDERSTATEMENT OF THE YEAR!

It felt really good to laugh with Amy, especially about something that has been so bad. Maybe all of this will work itself out after all.

April 18

I have been working on my AA steps so much that I haven't had much chance to journal! Doing the steps involves a lot of writing about a lot of different stuff, mainly about the people you resent, and what your part is in those resentments. Eventually I'll have to make a list of people I've hurt by drinking and using drugs so that I can make amends to them, but that's later, and Amy says not to worry about that yet.

Anyway, here's what's been going on:

1. I've been talking to my parents and to Amy on the phone every day.

2. Things are rocky with Mom and Dad. Mom still cries every time she talks to me. Dad is really quiet, like he doesn't know if he can still trust me. They're getting ready for Cam's big graduation party, even though it isn't until next month.

3. I've been allowed to check my e-mail a couple of times. Ross sent one e-mail that said he was sorry about everything that happened. Lauren sent an e-mail saying she was sorry that my parents shipped me to Palm Springs. She said that school is lame without me. I wrote both of them back and told them all about my rehab and Amy and how I felt really good about the changes I was making. I told them that I hope they check out some other AA meetings back in LA. I said that it made a big difference when I heard someone who was our age talk about addiction.

4. I'm working on Step 2 right now with Amy: "Came to believe that a Power greater than ourselves could restore us to sanity." Amy told me that Albert Einstein once said that "insanity" is "doing the same thing over and over again and expecting different results." I realized that's exactly what I'd done: continued to drink and do drugs and hang out with the people who did those things with me, even after I started getting into trouble.

I want to do things DIFFERENTLY now.

I finally feel like I have so much to look forward to. One of the guys in our group therapy told me that now I'm on a "pink cloud." It's this term in recovery that means I'm really happy and I think everything is going to be just perfect now.

I don't think everything is going to be perfect now.

But I sure do feel better.

April 27

Mom and Dad and Cam were here for family night tonight. It was hard to face them, but the looks on their faces when I asked their forgiveness for the way I treated them for the past year—for the lies, and the craziness—well, that made everything worth it.

Tomorrow I get to go home with them. I'll have been here for 28 days. It will be sad not seeing Amy as often, but she'll be moving to college this fall, and she's promised that we'll talk every day on the phone as long as I check in with her the way you're supposed to when you have a sponsor. We're getting ready to start on Step 4, which is a big list of all the people and places and ideas that I've ever resented in my life. The step says to make "a fearless moral inventory." It's actually really scary, but Amy said not to be scared of it, just to do it. There are really specific instructions about how to write it out in the Alcoholics Anonymous Big Book. She sat down with me by the pool the other day and made a little chart in my notebook with 4 columns so that I have a guide of how to do it.

I can't wait to get back home and share what I've learned with Lauren and Ross. I e-mailed both of them this week about going to meetings together when I get back home. I haven't had a chance to check my e-mails yet, but I'm excited that I can share what I've learned in my time here with them.

When I got here, I wasn't sure that I'd ever feel hopeful again. I felt like all of the good times of my life were over—behind me. I didn't want to even think about the idea of NEVER being able to party again.

Now I feel like I have everything to look forward to if I just don't drink or use a drug TODAY. If I can just remember that I only have to worry about TODAY, nothing seems so terrible or overwhelming.

April 28

I'M BACK HOOOOOOOOOOOOOOOOOOME!

You know, I never realized how BEAUTIFUL our house is, or how BIG my bedroom is. After living in an old motel in the desert for a month, I walked in and our place looks like a PALACE. I stood on the back balcony for a while and stared out at the ocean. Mom came up and stood behind me and wrapped her arms around me. Then she whispered into my ear how proud of me she was.

She said, You're a different girl now. I can see it in your eyes.

I got goose bumps when she said it. I felt tears come into my eyes, and I squeezed her fingers in mine, and I said, Yes, Mom. I AM different.

Later . . .

Dad just gave me back my cell phone! He said he and Mom discussed it and they can't believe the difference in me. I gave him a big hug and kissed him on the cheek.

I am going to yoga with Cam tonight for the first time in over a MONTH! I am so excited. I have to go grab my mat and get changed. Cam hates to be late.

Later . . .

Ross was at yoga! It was so good to see him!

When I walked into the room, he came running over and gave me a hug. We talked about what rehab was like for a little bit after class. I asked him how Lauren was, and he said she was okay, that they really missed me at school.

I told him Mom had sent my books to me and I had been doing as much schoolwork as I could at rehab but that I was still way behind, and I'd need his help to get caught up. He smiled his crooked little smile and said, I'm glad you're okay.

I hugged him tight and said, I'm more than okay. I'm better than ever. See you Monday.

Teen Found Dead of Accidental
Overdose, Coroner Rules

May 5th, _____—The 16-year-old girl whose body was recovered from a _____ beach house by police late Friday evening died of an accidental overdose the _____ County sheriff-coroner has declared.

The man whose father owned the house, Blake _____, 20, and his friend Ian _____, 21, were both retained for questioning in the matter. Two teenage friends of the victim, a boy and girl who were present at the scene but whose names have not been released, were also taken into juvenile custody.

Toxicology reports indicate that the young woman, the daughter of a local college professor and his wife, had taken lethal intravenous doses of crystal methamphetamine and heroin. Two journals found in the young woman's bedroom have been turned over to detectives by her parents.

A spokesman for the district attorney's office would not speculate on whether or not criminal charges would be filed in the case, but a full investigation is under way.

TURN THE PAGE FOR

A GLIMPSE AT TWO NOVELS

BY AMY REED

CLEAN

KELLY

My skin looks disgusting. Seriously, it's practically green. I have big gray bags under my eyes, my hair is all thin and frizzy, and I'm erupting all over the place with giant greasy zits. I look like a cross between a zombie, a hair ball, and a pepperoni pizza. Have I always looked like this? Was I just too high to notice?

OLIVIA

Did I pack my AP Chemistry book? I can't remember if I packed it. I am not ready for this. I am so not ready.

EVA

This place is a body. The walls are its bones or its skin, or both—an exoskeleton, like a crab has. A crab's shell is meant to keep it safe, to protect it from the world; it is made to keep things out. But this shell is meant to keep us in, to protect the world from us. We are cancerous cells. Quarantined. An epidemic. We are rogue mutations that cannot make contact with the outside world. We're left in here to bump around like science experiments. They watch us pee into cups. They study our movements. One doctor says, "Look, that one's slowing down. There may be hope." Another says, "No. They're all doomed. Let's just watch them burn themselves out."

CHRISTOPHER

Everyone's looking at me weird. They probably just had a secret meeting where they voted on how lame they think I am, and the verdict was "very lame." Add that to the fact that they can all most likely read my mind, and basically I'm doomed.

JASON

Fuck you fuck you fuck you FUCK YOU.

EVA

And the halls are like tongues, fingers, toes, like so many appendages. Dislocated. And these rooms are the lungs—identical, swollen, polluted. This one is the stomach, churning its contents into something unrecognizable.

CHRISTOPHER

That's it. They all got together and compared notes and have unanimously decided to look at me weird.

JASON

If I don't get a cigarette soon, I'm going to fucking kill somebody. We can smoke in here, right? They said we could smoke in here.

KELLY

They took everything, including my astringent. Now how the hell am I supposed to clean my face? Do they really think I'm going to *drink* astringent?

EVA

All these rooms—body parts with mysterious names and functions.

OLIVIA

When was the last time they cleaned this place?

JASON

Fuck this place.

BEAUTIFUL

I don't see her coming.

I am looking at my piece of pizza. I am watching pepperoni glisten. It is my third day at the new school and I am sitting at a table next to the bathrooms. I am eating lunch with the blond girls with the pink sweaters, the girls who talk incessantly about Harvard even though we're only in seventh grade. They are the kind of girls who have always ignored me. But these girls are different than the ones on the island. They think I am one of them.

She grabs my shoulder from behind and I jump. I turn around. She says, "What's your name?"

I tell her, "Cassie."

She says, "Alex."

She is wearing an army jacket, a short jean skirt, fishnet stockings, and combat boots. Her hair is shoulder length, frizzy and green. She's tall and skinny, not skinny like a model but skinny like a boy. Her blue eyes are so pale they don't look human and her eyelashes and eyebrows are so blond they're almost white. She is not pretty, not even close to pretty. But there's something about her that's bigger than pretty, something bigger than smart girls going to Harvard.

It's only my third day, but I knew the second I got here that this place was different. It is not like the island, not a place ruled by good girls. I saw Alex. I saw the ninth grade boys she hangs out with, their multicolored hair, their postures of indifference, their clothes that tell everybody they're too cool to care. I heard her loud voice drowning everything out. I saw how other girls let her cut in front of them in line. I saw everyone else looking at her, looking at the boys with their lazy confidence, everyone looking and trying not to be seen.

I saw them at the best table in the cafeteria and I decided to change. It is not hard to change when you were never anything in the first place. It is not hard to put on a T-shirt of a band you overheard the cool kids talking about, to wear tight jeans with holes, to walk by their table and make sure they see you. All it takes is moving off an island to a suburb of Seattle where no one knows who you were before.

"You're in seventh grade." She says this as a statement.

"Yes," I answer.

The pink-sweater girls are looking at me like they made a big mistake.

"Where are you from?" she says.

"Bainbridge Island."

"I can tell," she says. "Come with me." She grabs my wrist and my plastic fork drops. "I have some people who want to meet you."

I'm supposed to stand up now. I'm supposed to leave the pizza and the smart girls and go with the girl named Alex to the people who want to meet me. I cannot look back, not at the plate of greasy pizza and the girls who were almost my friends. Just follow Alex. Keep walking. One step. Two steps. I must focus on my face not turning red. Focus on breathing. Stand up straight. Remember, this is what you want.

The boys are getting bigger. I must pretend I don't notice their stares. I cannot turn red. I cannot smile the way I do when I'm nervous, with my cheeks twitching, my lips curled all awkward and lopsided. I must ignore the burn where Alex holds my wrist too tight. I cannot wonder why she's holding my wrist the way she does, why she doesn't trust me to walk on my own, why she keeps looking back at me, why she won't let me out of her sight. I cannot think of maybes. I cannot think of "What if I turned around right now? What if I went the other way?" There is no other way. There is only forward, with Alex, to the boys who want to meet me.

I am slowing down. I have stopped. I am looking at big sneakers on ninth grade boys. Legs attached. Other things. Chests, arms, faces. Eyes looking. Droopy, red, big-boy eyes. Smiles. Hands on my shoulders. Pushing, guiding, driving me.

"James, this is Cassie, the beautiful seventh grader," Alex says. Hair shaved on the side, mohawk in the middle, face pretty and flawless. This one's the cutest. This one's the leader.

"Wes, this is Cassie, the beautiful seventh grader." Pants baggy, legs spread, lounging with arms open, baby-fat face. Not a baby, dangerous. He smiles. They all smile.

Jackson, Anthony. I remember their names. They say, "Sit down." I do what they say. Alex nods her approval.

I must not look up from my shoes. I must pretend I don't feel James's leg touching mine, his mouth so close to my ear. Don't see Alex whispering to him. Don't feel the stares. Don't hear the laughing. Just remember what Mom says about my "almond eyes," my "dancer's body," my "high cheekbones," my "long neck," my hair, my lips, my breasts, all of the things I have now that I didn't have before.

"Cassie," James says, and my name sounds like flowers in his mouth.

"Yes." I look at his chiseled chin. I look at his teeth, perfect and white. I do not look at his eyes.

"Are you straight?" he says, and I compute in my head what this question might mean, and I say, "Yes, well, I think so," because I think he wants to know if I like boys. I look at his eyes and know I have made a mistake. They are green and smiling and curious, wanting me to answer correctly. He says, "I mean, are you a good girl? Or do you do bad things?"

"What do you mean by bad things?" is what I want to say, but I don't say anything. I just look at him, hoping he cannot read my mind, cannot smell my terror, will not now realize that I do not deserve this attention, that he's made a mistake by looking at me in this not-cruel way.

"I mean, I noticed you the last couple of days. You seemed like a good girl. But today you look different."

It is true. I am different from what I was yesterday and all the days before that.

"So, are you straight?" he says. "I mean, do you do drugs and stuff?"

"Yeah, um, I guess so." I haven't. I will. Yes. I will do anything he wants. I will sit here while everyone stares at me. I will sit here until the bell rings and it is time to go back to class and the girl named Alex says, "Give me your number," and I do.

. . .

Even though no one else talks to me for the rest of the day, I hold on to "beautiful." I hold on to lunch tomorrow at the best table in the cafeteria. Even though I ride the bus home alone and watch the marina and big houses go by, there are ninth grade boys somewhere who may be thinking about me.

Even though Mom's asleep and Dad's at work, even though there are still boxes piled everywhere from the move, even though Mom's too sad to cook and I eat peanut butter for dinner, and Dad doesn't come home until the house is dark, and the walls are too thin to keep out the yelling, even though I can hear my mom crying, there is a girl somewhere who has my number. There are ninth grade boys who will want it. There are ninth grade boys who may be thinking about me, making me exist somewhere other than here, making me something bigger than the flesh in the corner of this room. There is a picture of me in their heads, a picture of someone I don't know yet. She is not the chubby girl with the braces and bad perm. She is not the girl hiding in the bathroom at recess. She is someone new, a blank slate they have named beautiful. That is what I am now: beautiful, with this new body and face and hair and clothes. Beautiful, with this erasing of history.